He was blue-eyed and naked, as many of his dead predecessors had been . . . a carnivore with unkempt black hair that covered his forehead and ears and grew thickly down the back of his neck.

He looked as if he'd dropped down out of the Stone Age, but he hadn't. He had come from the future . . . come from battling a deadly, technologically advanced enemy sophisticated and insidious enough to hurl him back in time.

He opened his eyes slowly, let the doctor touch him. Then he saw Jeanmarie, and without warning brutally slammed her against the cabin.

Suddenly Highsmith had his answer. The warrior's sworn enemy in the future . . . was WOMAN!

"Once in a while, we can have aliens who are really human; and yet the difficulty of contact and understanding is as real as in any story of far-off worlds. ICE AND IRON is a fine example!"

—ANALOG

Books by Wilson Tucker

ICE AND IRON

THIS WITCH

THE WARLOCK

A PROCESSION OF THE DAMNED

LAST STOP

TO THE TOMBAUGH STATION

THE LINCOLN HUNTERS

THE MAN IN MY GRAVE

WILD TALENT

THE TIME MASTERS

CITY IN THE SEA

THE STALKING MAN

THE HIRED TARGET

TIME BOMB

THE SCIENCE-FICTION SUB-TREASURY

THE LONG LOUD SILENCE

RED HERRING

THE DOVE

THE CHINESE DOLL

TO KEEP OR KILL

THE YEAR OF THE QUIET SUN

ICE
&
IRON

Wilson Tucker

Ice and iron cannot be welded.
—Robert Louis Stevenson
The Weir of Hermiston

BALLANTINE BOOKS • NEW YORK

For Anne and Robert,
who know a moraine when they see one

Copyright © 1974, 1975 by Wilson Tucker

Library of Congress Catalog Card Number: 74-9146

SBN 345-24660-8-150

This edition published by arrangement with
Doubleday & Company, Inc.

First Printing: October, 1975

Cover Painting by Darrell Sweet

Printed in the United States of America

BALLANTINE BOOKS
A Division of Random House, Inc.
201 East 50th Street, New York, N.Y. 10022
Simultaneously published by
Ballantine Books, Ltd., Toronto, Canada

ONE

Ice

His name was Fisher Yann Highsmith and he was sometimes called "the Fisherman," but that cognomen had no heavenly connotation; he wasn't all that godly. Highsmith was too tall, too thin, and too bony to cast a decent shadow before the sun, but the sun was seldom seen this close to the glacier and shadows were among the things left behind in the warm southern states. His two most persistent problems were getting his long legs and big feet in and out from under desks and workbenches and standing upright outdoors in gale winds off the glacier.

Fisher Yann Highsmith picked up an object from his bench and held it up to the camera for inspection.

The woman on the phone promptly demanded: "What is *that*?" She had some difficulty focusing on the object and Highsmith wondered if she were skimming or shooting.

He said patiently: "A mud brick."

"Fisher, are you playing with bricks?"

"I'm playing with this one: one genuine mud brick, handmade, which looks exactly like the handmade mud bricks from Mesopotamia seven or eight thousand years ago. Furthermore, it has grass clinging to its bottom. Isn't *that* remarkable? The brick was found here—in this state, this year—but it doesn't belong here, it doesn't belong to this century. It's alien. I'm working on the problem."

"Fisher, I *don't* understand you."

"This old brick was found out there on the snowfield a few weeks ago, where mud bricks have no right to be. It had only a thin layer of new snow on top, so it's a

1

new artifact, if you read me. Now me, I'm a recon man —I'm supposed to build something with this brick, and explain that grass stuck on the bottom. But I'm stuck too."

The pouting image on the pictophone stared at him and the brick with complete lack of understanding. The image was irked by his stubborn refusal to surrender to her and by her inability to focus on the brick.

"But *this* will be a fun glow!" she protested. "We are having a *wonderful* party in Billings tonight. The city is to be abandoned and we're giving *it* a farewell party. It will be lost forever under the ice!"

"Billings won't be under ice for another fifty or a hundred years," Fisher said. "Take your time."

"*Are* you coming to my party?"

He shook his head for the watching camera. "No. I'm sorry, but no, not tonight. We're working tonight."

"You are *always* working," the woman's voice and image complained. "The *last* time I called you were working, and the time before *that*, and the time—"

Fisher broke in on her complaint. "I was working then and I'm working now; I'm working on this old brick. I've told you before that the team is tied up here, and we're likely to be tied up for weeks—perhaps months. We're waiting for Seventeen to fall."

The image hesitated, not quite ready to believe him. "That sounds like a flight or something."

"That will be a corpse," Fisher corrected her. "A body, quite dead, out there on the snowfileds. We've already picked up sixteen of them, and all the signs say the next one is coming. It could be any time."

The woman's image made a bad face. "How ghoulish! *You* are willing to pass up a wonderful glow party for a . . . a corpse?" She peered at him with frank disbelief. "Fisher, the government pays you to do *that?*"

He shifted his legs under the bench, seeking a more comfortable position. "An agency of the government pays me to do that—and they'd like to see some results. The agency is intrigued by the sudden appearance of sixteen dead men out there in the snow, men who lack the proper identification, men who sometimes lack clothing, men who just drop down out of the sky. The agency is puzzled by the bricks and the other things we find in the snow; the agency has several teams working on the problem, and I'm a member of one such team— we're working tonight, right here, now. I can't leave."

The woman's image tried once more. "Fisher, this will be a lovely, *lovely* glow, a farewell party. Several important people are coming to say goodbye to Billings, several important *air* people. You can meet them."

His patience was wearing away. "I don't care for glow parties, I don't care for air people. You know I don't smoke—I don't drop nor shoot nor skim, I'm a square peg. Your important fun people would hate me."

"But you *drink*," she reminded tartly. "You have that on saving grace. You could bring along that awful stuff you make and drink, that . . . that . . ."

"That bourbon."

"Bourbon, yes. *That* would be amusing."

"Will you and your fun people drink some bourbon?"

"Fisherman! That terrible stuff?"

He grinned at her unsteady image, quickly pleased at some secret humor. "Thank you for the invitation."

"Then you *aren't* coming?"

"I'm not coming—not tonight, not tomorrow, and not Tuesday, if the next day *is* Tuesday. I'm not sure any more, I've lost track of the calendar. Old Seventeen is due to drop, all the signs are right, and I don't want to miss him. I've waited too long."

The frustrated image attempted to peer around him and beyond him into the ready room, but the pictophone lens was aimed only at Highsmith. The room was no more than an indistinct blur to the woman on the phone, and not even the man knitting on the floor immediately behind Highsmith was visible to the scanning lens. The sounds of the knitting needles were so faint as to be inaudible to the microphone and she couldn't know he was there.

"What signs?" she demanded. "Where?"

He gestured toward a frosty window not visible to the

lens or the woman. "The incoming debris, that junk coming down out there. Our search parties are finding new debris north of here, between this base and the glacier, funny stuff like bricks and bits of cloth and shards of something else—all of it floating down from the sky. It just appears overnight on the snowfields. That kind of debris always precedes a man—well, almost always. *Sometimes* we draw a blank."

And again: "But that is ghoulish!" The irritated image studied him. "Where is it coming from?"

Highsmith shrugged. "Where, indeed? A number of fussy old bureaucrats in Washington South keep asking that question and we always give them the same answer."

"Don't tease me! What answer?"

Fisher again held the brick up to the lens and turned it about, as if seeking a trademark. "I always say, we're working on the problem."

Her image stared at his with exasperation. "Fisher!" The woman made a sudden jerky movement and the picture blanked out, dwindling to a faint jot of light somewhere in the center of the screen. A tinkling chime gave signal to a cleared channel and the phone was dead.

Fisher Yann Highsmith put down the brick and fell back in his chair in a posture of easy relaxation. He stretched out his legs until his feet struck the wall behind the bench, then clasped his hands behind his head and rocked. The chair moved with him in an equally easy motion, gently depressing itself to accommodate his spine and bony shoulders. They rocked together for a time.

He said aloud: "Ostrich feathers."

The man on the floor behind him muttered. "What?"

"Somebody had this chair stuffed with ostrich feathers. That's why if fits me so well."

"Ostriches have been extinct for fifty years."

"Imitation ostrich feathers," Fisher said.

It was a cushy, comfortable chair—something a flight controller or a briefing officer had left behind when the airfield was abandoned, and he much preferred it to writhing on the floor with a girl at a glow, even when in company with his amusing bourbon. Luxury. The softly lighted ready room behind him was quiet but for the soft sounds of the knitting needles and the gentle snoring of the only remaining pilot. The last pilot always slept and always snored; Highsmith couldn't remember seeing him awake except when they were traveling. He wondered now if so much sleep was unhealthy.

Another idle speculation blossomed in mind and he fell to wondering if the day after tomorrow *was* Tuesday? Had the woman really invited him to a Sunday-evening glow to mark the passing of Billings as an inhabited city? Was *today* Sunday, and *this* Sunday evening? Memory refused a ready answer. She had called him the first time with the first invitation on . . . on . . . what date?

Oh, yes: the same day Jeanmarie had marked the map. The big map, their operations map.

A detailed map of the empty, frigid northwestern states was spread out on the bench before him, but like the man on the floor it hadn't been visible to the picto-phone camera. Jeanmarie had marked that map the same day the first invitation was phoned in—the day of his first refusal. Highsmith bent forward to peer at the map, to study Jeanmarie's markings. She had used red ink.

Seven square sections of the operations map had been marked off to pinpoint the seven most recent falls, the locations of new debris coming down in their area. There were four compact locations in Saskatchewan, two others in Manitoba, and one smaller patch in Montana: seven in all, seven recent sites. As yet nothing had been found in Alberta or North Dakota but search teams were already standing by in those states. The map also bore a small red circle that marked their base of operations, an abandoned military airfield near Regina, and then finally a rough and ragged red line north of the base that reached from a point in the Rocky Mountains to another point in the waters of Hudson Bay. *That* red line represented the leading edge of the ice sheet, the oncoming glacier.

Highsmith thought it was too damned close.

He studied the map again for the hundredth time and guessed the most likely target would be somewhere in Saskatchewan—some desolate point between Regina and the ice shelf. Four of the falls were located in that rough area and they had yielded the largest amount of booty—if mud bricks and cloth and sticks and stones could be termed booty. *He* considered it booty, and if the deskmen in Washington South thought otherwise that was their tough luck. They were boobs living a life of warm ease. All they ever did down there was sit around on their fat wallets and bask in the—

"What's the temperature down in Virginia today?"

"Fisherman, I don't know that."

"Didn't anyone have the word in the mess hall?"

"I don't know, I wasn't there."

"I never knew you to miss a meal, Harley."

"Didn't you see the menu? Didn't you?"

"No."

"Spinach and beans and poor dog—again."

Highsmith said: "I wasn't there either."

He reached across his bench to the pictophone panel and punched for the control tower. A burly communications sergeant inhabited that tower just above the ready room, maintaining their links with the warmer world to the south. The sergeant's image appeared on the screen and solemnly considered Highsmith.

The image said reprovingly: "You should have gone to that party, Fisherman. Girls and dope!"

"You listened in! You watched!" Highsmith cried.

The image nodded easily. "I always do. There's nothing else to do around here." It peered at Highsmith.

"I've a notion to report you to the security officer," Highsmith retorted.

"I *am* the security officer."

"Then to hell with it. You wouldn't receive my complaint. What is the temperature in Washington South?"

The sergeant blinked only once. "At noon today it was twenty-one point one, Centigrade."

"Wow, that's hot!"

"I could do with some of it here, Fisherman."

"Both of us." He broke the connection and the screen image died away. Without turning he said: "Imagine that, Harley. All the way up to twenty-one or so!"

"Wow, that's hot," was the colorless echo.

Highsmith let his gaze drift to the red ice line on Jeanmarie's map, and then along to the mud brick resting on the map's margin. He knew the exact size of that brick because he'd measured it several times, and he knew the crack running along the middle of it because he'd cemented two matching pieces together to form the whole artifact: one complete mud brick, handmade, late Mesopotamian type, but with bits of non-Mesopotamian grass clinging to the bottom of it. The brick had been found only finger-deep in snow on the Saskatchewan border below the town of Lloydminster—a very fresh fall. The artifact was sixteen thousand kilometers and eight or nine centuries out of place. The fool thing had no *right* to be there, none of the debris had a right to be where it was found—and old Seventeen, when he finally fell, would be as sorely misplaced as the rest of it. Barfooted men didn't *belong* to the snowfields, didn't *belong* to the glacier. They lacked a decent identification. Bureaucrats down in Washington South nagged him about that while they sat around on their fat wallets and basked in heat waves. Twenty-one point one at noon today!

Aloud: "Well, I'm working on the problem."

After a while the man sitting on the floor behind him spoke. "You've lost a girl friend, Fisherman. You have. She won't call you again."

Highsmith agreed. He put his head back into his clasped hands and stared at the inert screen above the bench. The darkened glass seemed to rekindle the woman's pouting image in his mind, an imperfect image which flickered briefly and went out.

"No loss to me, Harley, no loss at all. I don't like her glow parties, I don't like her important air people, I don't like the crowds she generates: not for me. Everybody gets loose, everybody makes snakes on the floor, everybody experiments with each other. But I'm old-fashioned, did you know that? I don't fit in." He shifted his legs, preparing to move. "I like my own bourbon, I like female singles in the privacy of my own room or whatever, I like—" His hand unclasped to form a shaped gesture in the air. "That's what I like."

"You're anachronistic," Harley said.

Highsmith agreed again. "Old-fashioned, antisocial, anachronistic, that's me. Date me in the last century."

"She *does* seem to be hurrying the city to its grave. She does."

"Farewell to Billings," Highsmith mocked. "That's poppycock. Billings won't go under for a long time yet; they won't begin moving the people out for another year or so, and they won't actually abandon for ten or twenty."

"Do you really make your own bourbon?"

"I do indeed, and I've got a federal license for it. It's fast becoming a lost art, Harley."

"Is it expensive?"

"Not very expensive."

"What's it like?"

"Smooth, mellow, and full of thunder."

The voice behind him said: "Maybe I'll try it sometime. Maybe I will."

Highsmith carefully pulled his long legs from under the bench and revolved in the chair, taking care not to bang his knees on the supports. He faced the ready room. The pilot was sleeping and snoring on a cot wedged into a corner of the room and the two adjoining walls of that corner seemed to amplify the sounds; he slept in his clothing with his boots beside him on the floor. Near at hand, at the bench next to Highsmith's own, an empty chair and a stack of books awaited the return of the young woman who had left the room on the run nearly an hour ago. She hadn't offered an explanation. In the middle of some now forgotten conversation Jeanmarie had simply closed a book, spun around, and darted from the room.

In the exact center of the ready room beneath the one really bright light, an older man sat cross-legged on the floor industriously knitting a shapeless garment. He peered closely at the task, squinting through the lower lenses of his bifocals to see the stitching. The glasses had slipped down the ridge of his nose and now threatened to drop off into his lap. The man was bald and shiny under the light, and wore a sloppy pullover sweater that may have been a product of his own needles. The four of them were the core of the Saskatchewan team: the sleeping pilot, the absent woman, the knitting man, and Fisher Yann Highsmith.

"Harley, do you *do* anything?"

The man on the floor hesitated and squinted up at him before catching his meaning. "Oh, I skim once in a while, I skim. But not often; it affects one's centrality, robs one of the ability to concentrate. That young woman was skimming, she couldn't focus on you." The garment was put down for a moment. "Now, think of it: the patient would be rather unhappy if I performed an appendectomy while in that condition, wouldn't he? Wouldn't he?"

"He'd probably be dead."

"Or a terribly mixed up man," Harley said. "What was the point of your question?"

"You won't like my bourbon. It dosen't mix very well with some drugs, most drugs."

"It doesn't?"

"I've heard some scary stories."

"But I haven't read about that in my literature." The needles resumed their labors on the garment.

"There's hardly enough bourbon around to get into your literature. My license number is only sixty-three."

"Then so much for that; I *won't* try it sometime. No, I won't; I need a clear head. Why didn't you tell your party girl what I tell my wife?"

"I didn't know you were married."

"Well, I *am*; most men my age are." The needles and the shapeless garment were lifted into the air and jabbed in a vague direction indicating south. The man looked at the south wall. "She's in Mexico. My wife and I were relocated to Mexico when the ice came."

"Harley, I didn't know you lived up *here*."

An easy nod. "Not far from here, not far at all. We lived in Churchill, I had a good practice in Churchill; that was a nice little town over on the western shore of Hudson Bay." Harley's gaze was still fixed on the south wall of the room. "We were relocated when the ice reached the Egg River. I lost a good practice, a good home, my own saddle horse, lost it all. The ice drove us out. I miss her."

"Your wife or the horse?"

"My wife, of course."

"Harley, are you rich?"

"No."

"Only rich men can afford horses these days."

"Nonsense."

Highsmith looked down on him and realized he didn't know the team doctor very well; he hadn't known the man was a wealthy, married northlander before the coming of the glacier—and despite the disclaimer he was suddenly convinced the doctor *was* rich: only the rich could afford the rarity of a horse. But for that matter he didn't know any of his companions very well, didn't know where they lived or what they'd done, because the team had been fitted together in a hurry and flown to Saskatchewan with a minimum of social amenities. They had found a caretaker force left behind when the airfield was abandoned, and before long even that crew would be pulled out.

"Is Jeanmarie married?"

"I don't know. I didn't ask."

"Is she rich?"

"Fisherman, *I* don't know that."

"How long have you known her?"

"The same as you: a week, or two, or three. How long have we been together here?"

"I guess a week, or two, or three."

"So it doesn't matter, it doesn't. We'll stay as long as there is work to do, and then go elsewhere. I'll go elsewhere, I expect to stay with the ice up here."

"That glacier scares me."

"When did you see it?"

"I haven't yet."

Harley peered up over the tops of his glasses for a long surly moment and abruptly went back to his knitting. A silence grew between them. Highsmith waited, patiently at first and finally with some annoyance. He tapped his feet on the floor to gain the doctor's attention.

"Harley, what *do* you tell your wife?"

"I tell her about the dead men coming in on us."

"I did that much, but what do you *say*?"

"Whenever she complains of my absences, my long absences, I tell her: 'They are coming in like stragglers from a lost battle, like flotsam from some great unknown disaster.' Rather poetic, wouldn't you say?" He looked up once more. "Now, wouldn't you?"

"I guess I would. What does she say?"

"She always asks what I mean by that."

"What *do* you mean by that?"

"Fisherman, poets need not explain their creations."

Fisher Highsmith looked at the sky with surprise and open delight: he could see stars. A full moon was visible through a break in the cloud cover and it worked white magic on the snowy distances, reminding him of a painted winter scene that used to hang on the wall of his boyhood home. Something moved in the frigid moonlight, some small animal the size of a starving runty dog ran along the fence encircling the base seeking a means of entry. He guessed a wolf or a lynx. The Saskatchewan team had been warned to find an incoming body before the wolves did. Highsmith pressed his nose against the frosted window and watched the furtive animal until it vanished from sight around a far corner of the fence. There was no other movement, but yet he stared at the corner and beyond it: the dark-shaped mass of Regina lay off that corner, a ghost city given up to the enemy.

Regina was but one of the many cities and towns abandoned to the enemy. Above the old Trans-Canada Highway, now renamed USNA-1 and already threatened with obliteration, all of Alberta, Saskatchewan, Manitoba, and most of Ontario were practically deserted —swept clear by troops and left to the prowling wolves and the oncoming ice sheets. The Yukon and the Northwest Territories had been under for nearly a century. The people of the old Canadian states had been resettled in the south along the Gulf Coast and on land purchased from Mexico, all driven out by the new glaciation grinding down from the Arctic. Behind them they left Regina, left the cities and towns unlit, unheated, uninhabited: a place for wolves. Many of those places had been abandoned before he was born.

Below the starry sky, below that brilliant moon, the view from his window was miserable.

A single aircraft waited on the runway, thirty spaces and a jump beyond the outer door. It was fueled and ready, with its mesotron engines always kept at proper operating temperature by means of an electric cable snaking across the snow from the shops. Highsmith had seen the pilot sprint across the runway, disconnect that cable before a shop mechanic could reach it, climb into the cabin to start the engines, and then turn on him with a pained *you're late* expression as he climbed through the cabin door. Excessive sleep seemed to provide the man with excessive speed and agility.

The shops were in an adjoining building out of his line of sight; the communications tower was directly over the ready room, where flight controllers had worked when this was a busy airfield; while the commissary and sleeping quarters were at the rear of the building in many scattered rooms once used for other purposes. The hospital—a room with two beds—was just down the corridor from the ready room. This single window, this one at the tip of Fisher's nose, gave him a view of the snowy runway, the waiting aircraft, a long section and corner of the fencing, the distant hulk of the ghost city, and an expanse of frigid prairie limited only by his vision under moonlight. Barren country. None but the search parties were out there now, picking up debris and waiting for the corpse of Seventeen. They prowled under permanent cloud cover and unending snow, often working within sight of the advancing glacier. The former Canadian states would soon be lost to history.

Highsmith thought it certain that the doctor's home town was now nothing more than rubbish and pulverized gravel rolling under the ice. In time that gravel would be deposited in some one of the southern states —in Minnesota or Iowa or Illinois—if the ice sheets continued their present course.

He said aloud: "Sixty-one meters per year."

"What?"

Highsmith turned from the window. "Jeanmarie said the ice was coming down on us at the rate of sixty-one meters per year. That almost sets a new record."

"Jeanmarie is a good polylib, one of the best. She *is*. You may rely on the figure."

Highsmith rapped his knuckles on the mud brick.

"Bully for her. I'm a good recon man, one of the best, but you can't rely on me. My shop is littered with bricks and pieces that won't form a pattern—any pattern. I haven't been able to construct an altar or an oven or somebody's doghouse, I can't make those damned bricks work for *me*. And I've got pieces of wood I *think* formed a bow but I can't fit together enough pieces to form any kind of a weapon. I haven't done *anything*, Harley."

When there was no immediate reply Fisher Highsmith sat down on the floor in front of the knitter and watched the intricate needle play for an impatient time. Knitting a garment seemed a tedious business at best.

"This base will be under ice when I'm halfway between Jeanmarie's age and yours, did you know that? It's time to move out of here, Harley."

"But we've just arrived, we have! We've been here only a few weeks, one or two or three, you said."

"You said it first."

Harley stopped work to peer at the reconstructionist. "Ah, you're joking. You are! Please hold up a little flag or make some signal when you joke. This base *will* be under ice before I learn to understand you, Fisherman."

"Comedians need not explain their creations."

The doctor spared him a sour glance.

Highsmith quoted: "They are coming in like strangers from a lost battle, like flotsam from an unknown disaster." He gestured toward the window. "The only disaster I see around here is the ice."

"Not that, not that! They aren't Eskimo bodies."

"Then whose bodies are they?"

"I'm tempted to say we're working on the problem."

"Do that, say that, and I'll go out to the shop and play with my bricks. I'm thinking of building a brick spaceship—the government could use one."

"Not spacers! They can't be spacers, they can't! We haven't put a ship into space since the Depression, not since the Treasury went bankrupt in the Depression. Those sixteen men had no cancerous tissue, they were never in space." He shook the needles at Highsmith. "And don't suggest the orbital platforms. You know those platforms are fully automated. No, they weren't spacers."

"But some of the bodies were burned."

"*Not* by solar raidation! They were groundlings, sixteen separate autopsies insist they were groundlings."

"They weren't Mesopotamian groundlings."

"Nor were they Mesopotamian spacers," Harley snapped. "I *know* the only natural disaster around is the glaciation, I know it. This is the only disaster, other than that Mississippi quake."

"Aw, that was twenty years ago. These bodies aren't quake victims."

"I didn't say they were, I *didn't.*"

"There aren't any wars going on." Highsmith pressed the point. "Nothing but that little squabble in Egypt."

"I *know* all this."

"So, then—?"

"So you didn't listen very well, Fisherman. That bourbon is rotting your fine mind. I said stragglers from a *lost* battle, flotsam from an *unknown* disaster."

"A lost battle? Harley, how can anyone misplace a battle?"

"The doctor lost his patience. "Go play with your mud bricks! Go build a mud igloo!" And he swung wildly with the garment and needles, intending a wicked swipe.

Highsmith lurched and rolled away across the floor, fearing the roundhouse swing of the needles. They would have cut deeply if they had connected. He was still rolling when the woman entered.

Jeanmarie pushed open the door with the toe of a boot and strode into the ready room holding a thick sheaf of papers that smelled of fresh ink. The young woman stopped in midstride to stare first at the doctor, and then with astonishment at Highsmith as he threw himself away. Knowing he had a new audience, Highsmith rolled all the way across the room and hurled himself against the wall with exaggerated mummery. The wall shook when he thumped against it.

The aircraft pilot awoke with a strangled snore and looked down at him over the end of his cot.

"Foul play!" Highsmith cried. "I've been stabbed!"

"Then leave her alone," the pilot retorted.

"Not her, you idiot! *Him.*"

The sleepy pilot looked at Jeanmarie and the doctor and then back to the man on the floor near his feet. "It serves you right. Doc is married."

Highsmith sat up and spun around on his backside to deliberately kick the supporting legs from under the cot. The lower end collapsed, with the pilot riding it to the floor to produce a second crash. The pilot balled a fist and put it under the Fisherman's nose.

Jeanmarie cried: "Stop it!"

The pilot blinked at her, looked to Highsmith and suggestively waggled the balled fist in his face, and then fell back on the canted cot to close his eyes in sleep. The angle seemed not to bother him at all.

Highsmith turned his attention to the woman after propping himself against the wall.

He asked: "What's new on the iceberg front?"

And got a prompt reply: "Pack ice has been sighted floating near the fiftieth parallel, with bergs as far south as Bermuda. The government is discussing the abandonment of deep-sea ports from Halifax down to Boston."

"Jeanmarie, please—I'm waving my little flag."

"I see no flag."

"Pretend you do. Harley wants me to wave a little flag when I make jokes or ask foolish questions. I just did." He indicatied the fresh print in her hand. "New traveling orders? Are we leaving already?"

She said no as she crossed to her bench and placed the sheaf of papers alongside the stack of books. "They did it for me, they were very prompt about it."

"Who did what for you?"

"Someone at the agency in Washington South located the book I wanted. They sent the first half along just now, and the sergeant's copier printed it for me." She glanced at him. "I overheard your party invitation."

"My whole life is paraded before other people's eyes," he complained. "That doesn't look like a book."

"It is the facsimile of a book. They couldn't send the original, of course; the original is very old, it was published about three hundred years ago and is now considered quite valuable. Someone borrowed a copy from the Library of Congress to make this facsimile."

"Ah, another old history book."

"I am not sure history is the proper term, but it is a strange and fascinating account of certain events of the past." She turned her chair around to face the room and sat down. "Harley, were you aware that falls were seen and recorded as long as three centuries ago? Perhaps as long as four centuries? Debris very similar to ours was reported in several states, and parts of Europe."

"A body count?" the doctor asked quickly.

"None apparently. The history doesn't record a body *per se*. There have been other reports of bodies found lacking identification, but those bodies were not connected with the falls of debris." She hesitated, then said: "I will offer an opinion. I think it entirely possible that bodies *were* found about the same time, but no one possessed the ready intelligence to associate them with the falls of other matter. The eighteenth, nineteenth, and twentieth centuries were dark ages in many respects and the peoples of those times were rather incognitive."

"Mud bricks?" Highsmith asked.

"None that have been recorded."

"Then what *did* fall?"

"Fish, frogs, water, sticks, stones, tree leaves, soil, and other materials the ancients failed to recognize. If this history may be believed, the ancients did not want to admit they had seen anything fall, and several of them took pains to explain away the unexplainable."

"Were they afraid? What did their governments do?"

"There was no line of organized research, and the governments of that day were inclined to ignore matters. It may have been fear of the unknown. Some few efforts were made to—"

She was interrupted by the jangling phone.

The first image seen was that of the communications sergeant in the tower above; he adjusted the camera to peer into the room. Fisher Highsmith came up off the floor like a released spring and cried out to the sleeping man. The pilot swung his feet over the edge of the cot and groped blindly for his boots.

The sergeant said: "I've got Search Three on line, Fisherman. They've picked up your old man." His image faded from the screen to be replaced by a visual "NP," which indicated a voice transmission without picture.

A distant voice shouted: "Fisherman?"

"Here!"

"This is Busby on Search Three. Congratulate us, we got here before the wolves did."

"Where? Where are you?"

"Two kilometers southeast of Lloydminster, on old Route Five. The old Fort Battleford road is under us. We have beacons out for you."

The pilot shouted. "Get the coordinates—get his position!" He was already sprinting for the door.

The shout was overheard. "Fifty-three degrees plus seventeen minutes north, one hundred and ten degrees west on the mark. Watch for our beacons."

The door slammed behind the racing pilot.

Jeanmarie said with alarm: "The ice has reached *that* position; Lloydminster is vacated. Are you on the ice, Search Three?"

"We're damned near under it, lady!" Busby retorted. "This is shelf ice here. Your man hit a shelf somewhere above and tumbled down on us—fell right on our heads. Come on and *move*, Fisherman, it's cold here!"

"What is the temperature?" Jeanmarie asked.

"Negative forty point something. Get moving!"

"We *are* moving," Highsmith shouted back. "Wrap the body in a thermal sack—don't let it freeze."

"We've got it in a sack! *All* the brainy people on this team aren't sitting around in cozy rooms having a good time on thirty dollars a month. Fisherman—?"

"He's not here," Highsmith shouter at the phone. "He left ten minutes ago for the cold blue yonder—he wants to keep that thirty-dollar job!"

TWO

Iron

The brickmaker came out of the frigid waters of the runoff pond and dropped a double handful of bottom mud on the beach. He thought he had enough. He'd been working the pond since sunrise, scooping up mud and laying it ashore to work later in the day, watching the mound build up to a reasonable height, and now he thought there was enough to build blinds on both sides of the hill.

A game trail wound up the other side of the hill, crossed the rocky ridge at his back, and led down this side in more direct fashion to the pond's edge. He'd discovered it only a few days ago and knew by the signs it was a rich trail as well as an old one. It meandered on the opposite side of the hill because the animals were following the scent of water, but it straightened and dropped more quickly on this side as the game sighted the pond. Food was plentiful along this trail and he judged it a place to build two blinds. This one should be near the water, a stone's throw, while the other should be near the top. The heavier animals would be tiring as they neared the top.

They could be taken as they slowed on the long uphill climb, near the rocks, and taken here at water's edge when they stooped to drink. There was no cover other than those rocks and they were misplaced for game hunting; all the hills offered nothing but weeds and tall grass for cover and that was not enough.

The brickmaker washed the mud from his hands in the cold water and then sprang up to stand ramrod still in the bright sun while he searched the horizons. Only his head and eyes moved, seeking intruders. He smelled the wind for scent of an enemy, listened to it for any telltale sound, and warily scanned the valley mouth for a moving thing. There was nothing but a flock of birds skimming the next ridge. When he was satisfied, the brickmaker retreated a safe distance from the beach and threw himself down in the high grass beside his weapons. The sun was high and warm and in a short while it would bake the chill out of his legs. The pond water was painfully cold and he was glad to be done with it.

The water in the pond was runoff, spillage from the great lake washing the northern end of the valley and the series of grass-covered hills. As cold as that runoff was, it was nothing to the deadly chill of the lake and the river which fed that lake. The river, the first water, rolled down from the ice wall in the far north and spilled into the lake, the second water.

Smaller rivers spewed out from the lake and dropped away through the other valleys like this one, but *this* one was dry and as grassy as the hills, having only a rivulet that dumped water into a series of ponds. He'd chosen this pond because the game trail was here, a rich trail showing age.

The best mud for mud bricks was found in ponds. That mud up on the lake bottom was poor building material, for it was mixed with sand and gravel coming down from the ice, and he'd learned with experience to avoid it. The icy water had nearly killed him and his body would not become accustomed to it. He'd built many game blinds as he walked the hills, always working east by south in pursuit of food and a warmer sun, and sometimes he stayed a very long time when he found a place and a trail as promising as this. His father had taught him to make bricks and build blinds long ago when they hunted together—so long ago that now he couldn't remember the man very well. Time had dimmed the image of him. His father had shown him the lack of cover on the plains and in the hills, the lack of trees and decent brush for hiding, but told him that game could not see a hunter lying in wait behind a wall. The blind need be only large enough to conceal a crouching man, and it would serve its purpose a very long time if the hunter took care not to leave his own marks around for the wary animal to find.

The brickmaker had first seen the ice when he was young, when he was small. His father was still alive on that day and the two of them had stood on a broad plain of grass and wildflowers, staring across the distance at the mighty wall of ice. It had been a warm day like this one; the sun was bright in the sky and there was no cold breath from the ice—not at this distance. His father had made him understand that the wall was going away from them, that once long ago it had covered the plain where they stood but now it was running away before the sun, as a deer runs from a charging cat. After the ice went away the grass came, and then wildflowers, and after them the game and the hunters trickled into the open places. The first water cut a wide, deep channel across the plain and dumped the melt into the second water, a lake so vast he'd walked many days along its shore, circling it to reach the valleyed hills beyond.

The brickmaker rolled over on his naked belly and reached for the breechcloth he'd taken from a dead man. It fitted too snugly but it was useful; it covered him and protected his belly when he crawled.

The breechcloth's original owner had made a mistake: he had supposed that he could help himself to meat the brickmaker had brought down that same day, he had thought he was stronger than the brickmaker and the food was for the taking. The thief realized his mistake too late.

The brickmaker profited well from the encounter.

He took the man's lance because it was better than his own, the point of the weapon being a wonderfully long and hardened bone of a kind he'd not seen before; he suspected it was the long tooth of an animal he'd never seen. He took the arrows because they were the equal of his, but the bow was cast aside as an inferior thing. The strip of cloth about the dead man's belly caught his fancy and he pulled it off to see what might be hidden there. No other weapon or treasure was revealed, but the brickmaker pulled the thing on over his own belly to learn that the snugness of it provided a new and unusual sensation. He liked the sensation, and kept it. And finally the body of the would-be thief provided meat for two days, until the odor of it caused him to throw the remains away.

He was on the ridge of the hill searching for rocks to form the molds when the sound reached him.

The brickmaker flattened his belly to the ground and waited, seeking the source of the sound. The wind was not helpful; boulders interfered, masking it, shunting it, and he was unable to pick out a betraying odor. Uneasy because of the loss, he began crawling through the rocks to a vantage point where he could look down on the pond.

Two of the enemy were in the valley.

The strange and heady scent of the enemy came to him now on the free wind, triggering a responsive alarm. He had always been frightened of them, of their scent, even when watching their passage from a safe distance. He knew them to be deadly. The two figures were but a short distance away upwind, but they hadn't yet found his sign or caught scent of him; they hadn't discovered the heaped mud beside the pond or seen the flattened grass bed where he had rested and dried in the sun. The brickmaker studied the pair as the first worms of panic turned in his mind, looking at their hands and their packs to learn if they carried the weapon that pushed things away, looking at their tight-belted waists to see how many ears hung there, and looking behind them to know if there were more. The scene at the valley mouth jolted him, frightened him, and the worms of panic raced through his mind. They were a company, a great horde on the move.

A body of the enemy was pouring into the valley— more than he could count by any number he knew, marching north at an easy pace along the floor and seemingly intent on the great lake at the other end of his valley. They would pass just below him, pass his hiding place *here* and his heaped mud down *there*, going upvalley to the second water. He couldn't fight them all but there was no wish to fight. He had lived this long because he knew when to stand his ground and when to flee.

As he watched, an astonishing thing came into view, a great thing he could not name or accurately describe because he'd never before seen one. It was long and big, and shaped strangely like his bricks, but unlike his bricks it had high sides and rounded corners—and it moved. He could not guess how. No one pulled it, pushed it, but it moved. One of the enemy sat atop it. It moved smoothly and silently over the valley floor on— There were things turning beneath it, round things which rolled on and on like a rock rolling downhill, leaving great wide, flattened trails in the grass behind. The thing moved without sound. The only sounds were the passage of the enemy, and their massed scent was heavy on the wind.

The brickmaker scrabbled away from his observation point and crawled over the rock-strewn ridge to the game trail winding down the opposite side. He knew only fear, and he gathered up his weapons to run. Those two scouts in the lead would find his heaped mud at any moment, and at their cry the hunt would be on. Both of the pair had carried the weapon that pushed things away —he couldn't stand against those, he wouldn't stand against even one.

His lance in one hand, the bow hanging over his arm and shoulder with a wicker basket of arrows bouncing on his naked back, the brickmaker bolted away from the ridge rocks and sped down the game trail past the point he'd chosen for his first blind. A furtive movement in the high grass below him registered on his consciousness as small game frightened away. He plunged on. The trail wandered, running from left to right and back again in no realistic fashion, and when he could he made short cuts, leaping through the grass to find it below him again on the next switchback. Beneath him a rabbit was routed from its shallow burrow, a small and equally frightened thing that ran blindly down the open trail a considerable distance before veering off into cover. The brickmaker raced on, running at breakneck speed but with an economy of breath.

He had no plan in mind when he reached bottom; he would simply keep running, running up or down this new valley, running toward or away from the second water, doing whatever seemed best when he reached the floor. Fear drove him downhill, fear would dictate the next decision at the bottom.

A distant cry went up behind him, a surprisingly loud cry in spite of the intervening ridge, and he knew his handiwork had been found. A shrill whistle followed the cry of discovery, and they were after him.

Now he was running more swiftly, blindly, ignoring

the switchbacks of the trail and plunging down the hill in almost a straight line. He charged through the high grass and nearly overran two more of the enemy lying there, one to either side of the trail waiting for him. The brickmaker felt shock, but never stopped running.

He could not stop his onward rush, had no desire to stop it, knew better than to stop it: he would destroy himself if he paused. They had tricked him—or he had tricked himself; he hadn't guessed they would send scouts up the adjoining valleys to protect their flanks, and he had dismissed the betraying movement in the grass as only some small animal. The wind had carried their scent away from him. The pair of them had jumped to their jeet and now they closed in for the kill. He thought they were laughing. He looked at their hands and looked at the grassy beds where they had lain, and he knew a sudden elation, a brief but genuine elation—they were not holding the weapons that pushed him. The black weapons rested on the grass behind them. Both of the enemy carried only the shining knives, the long blades that caught and reflected sunlight.

The brickmaker whipped up his lance and let his headlong momentum work for him. One stood on the trail, knife at ready, blocking his way. That one began a feint coupled with a side step. He turned slightly and rammed the lance through the unprotected body, the hardened tip tearing into the belly and bursting out the back. A scream of agony exploded in his ear and then they closed, the two of them falling together in a tangle of thrashing arms and legs. His opponent struck the ground first and the lance snapped off in his hands. The brickmaker threw himself away but he wasn't quite fast enough: a long blade caught him on his shoulder and slashed down the length of his arm to the elbow. His wicker basket broke under him and the arrows spilled out onto the ground. The bowstring was a burning thread twisted about his neck.

The standing enemy jumped at him and the brickmaker kicked out, wanting to break the legs and smash the kneecaps. He missed, kicked again as the enemy came back in, but succeeded only in delivering a stunning blow to the shin. He saw the hesitation and leaped. They grappled together and the scent stung his nostrils. Again that long knife raked him, the shining blade digging into his rib cage, searching for the heart. The brickmaker jumped back, drove his knee hard into the opposing groin, and as the enemy stumbled and gasped for breath he smashed the hand and wrist holding the knife. Deliberately then he picked up the fallen blade and cut the other's throat.

A cry was heard on the ridge, an angry cry that carried shrilly over the agonized screaming of the one on the ground at his feet—the one with the broken lance through the belly.

The brickmaker paused only long enough to snatch up the black thing on the grass, the strange black weapon that could push things away. He turned and ran for his life.

THREE

Ice

The runway was brilliantly white under the moon and the few artificial lights. Faces peered out of the shopwindows as Fisher Highsmith galloped from the door to the waiting aircraft. He climbed into the cabin.

The pilot was half turned in his seat, glaring at him with a pained expression as he clambered in. Jeanmarie and the doctor were already buckled into their seats, as the aircraft vibrated with a soft feathery trembling under the preheated engines. Highsmith buckled himself into his padded bucket and then plugged a dangling electric cord into an overhead receptacle; the snowsuit worn under his parka would feed off the energy from the aircraft's generator, warming him until he pulled free to go outside. Heater packs built into the snowsuits were of limited value and limited range; the search parties working the snowfields relied on portable generators mounted on their supply sleds.

Highsmith craned his neck to look back at Jeanmarie and the doctor.

In the next strangled moment he lost his breath and his stomach dropped into his bowels. He hadn't known they were moving, lifting off the runway. The pilot had shot forward only a scant few meters and then tilted his engines to rocket toward the moon. Highsmith gulped and clutched at his stomach. Behind him Harley fought for breath.

He said weakly: "Jeanmarie . . . ?"

"Yes?"

"What is the failure rate for vertical takeoffs?"

"Eight percent."

"Please tell that lunatic up front."

There was no reply, no response to the suggestion. The woman was hugging her stomach with lips pressed tight.

When the craft straightened out and moved forward on a horizontal plane Highsmith let out a great breath of free air and turned to the tiny window beside him, watching the northern rim of the world for a first glimpse of the hostile force he'd not yet seen: the new glaciation. The ice. Millions of metric tons of moving ice, moving down on *him*, but he'd seen only pictures of the enemy. There had been pictures on the newscasts for many years, since the years when he was young, particularly when some former Canadian town or national park was obliterated—but pictures were not the real thing, pictures were but images someone was seeing and relaying back to safer climes.

He'd seen pictures of the glaciation when he was a boy, and later when he was a young man in his teens; he had studied the pictures with a greater interest while he served his apprenticeship with the search parties combing Michigan and Wisconsin for debris, but he'd never seen the real thing in his lifetime—despite the nearness of the Regina base to the ice sheets. Only Search Three had ventured *that* far north. Highsmith knew better than to anticipate silvery ice rivers flowing in the moonlight: that kind of nonsense was for poets who wholly failed to grasp the enormity of the disaster, the bulk of the wall. Ice was destruction and death; the moving wall was an instrument of calamity. The real glaciation was a dark, burgeoning gray-black blanket of ice and mud and stone pushing down out of the Arctic refrigerator and over-running the adjoining states. Uncounted villages and towns were ground beneath it while uncounted cities were standing empty, awaiting their turn. The summer capital at Ottawa had been abandoned for the duration, and there was a belief it would fall beneath the ice.

The ice sheet had been there before he was born and he'd seen pictures before he learned to read, before he really understood what glaciation was. When he *had* learned to read, Highsmith acquired first knowledge of the enemy. Mean annual temperatures had been slipping long before his birth, since about 1950 at the old Canadian frontier stations, and by 1970 a marked decline was noted as far south as Chicago. In that winter the Great Lakes remained closed to shipping three weeks longer than any other year, due to persistent ice. In ten years more the transient snowline reached the Florida border regularly each January or February, and officials in Washington—the old Washington—publicly worried.

The Greenland icecap began expanding, slowly pushing coastal settlements off into the sea, and new measurements of the cap found the maximum ice thickness had increased by ninety meters. Dormant glaciers returned to life and crept down into the ancient piedmont plains of Alaska, following the ice paths of twelve thousand years earlier; the Bering Strait failed to melt free in the summer. Broken ice became a common sight in the Faeroe Islands.

Now—in this year, this day—the nothernmost United States, all former Canadian provinces, were deserted and given over to the caretaker troops, the search parties, and the wolf packs. The government had acknowledged defeat when it abandoned the summer capital at Ottawa.

Fisher Highsmith plucked at a name and a number deep in the recesses of his mind but they eluded him. He turned away from the small window.

"That was how many millions of years?"

Jeanmarie sensed his meaning.

"The Permian?"

"Yes—that's the one."

"The Permian has been estimated at about thirty million years, but that was not a continuous glaciation. There were frequent interglacial periods of warmth, of retreating ice and normalized climate. The Pleistocene has been measured at only about one million years thus far."

Highsmith said gloomily: "If *this* one lasts thirty million years, we're dead."

There was a suspicious sound from the doctor and Highsmith craned around to look. Harley was knitting.

Jeanmarie said: "There is no good reason to believe the world has advanced to a post-Pleistocene period. Most authorities agree on that."

"Jeanmarie, you're a pessimist."

"That isn't true."

"You are saying that we've got another twenty-nine million years to go—that *this* ice will last for another twenty-nine million. That isn't optimism."

"But I didn't say that!"

"She didn't say that," the doctor agreed.

Highsmith turned on the pilot. "Would *you* care to vote on the question?"

The pilot answered: "She didn't say that."

"All right, all right—I'll jump out now and leave the three of you alone. I'll walk home and you'll just have to stumble along without me. But before I go overboard, what did she say?"

"She said we may or may not be on the backside of the Pleistocene ice age," Harley said helpfully. "We may or may not be in for a prolonged glaciation. We may or may not endure this one for thirty million years."

"She didn't say that!" Highsmith cried.

"She didn't say that," the pilot agreed.

"Jeanmarie—"

Patiently: "The available evidence indicates that the world has endured only three ice ages, in the proper sense of the term: the first in late Pre-Cambrian times about six hundred million years ago, the second in early Permian about two hundred and fifty million years ago, and finally the present Pleistocene, which opened about one million years ago. Most authorities now believe we are still living in the Pleistocene glacial age; we have never left it. The events of the past century underscore that belief. The scant few thousand years of recorded history —our history—represent no more than a period of temporary warmth between glacial advances. That brief period of warmth is now ending."

"With twenty-nine million years ahead of us!"

"No."

"Why no?"

"The next interglacial period may be only five or ten thousand years away, or it may be twenty thousand."

"But the Pleistocene goes on!"

"Of course."

"And it *could* last twenty-nine million."

"Perhaps. No one will guess at the duration. The duration of previous ages has not been determined with satisfactory accuracy."

"I'll guess at it," Highsmith declared. "I'll give you a reading. It won't last twenty-nine or even thirty million years—that's *too* long, that's bad for business. It will last until we are old men, until everybody but Jeanmarie is an old man, and *then* it will stop when our lives are wasted. And all this funny stuff will stop with it: the debris and the bodies will stop falling and the agency will close out the shop and let us go home—go south. But we'll all be old men with wasted lives, except you, Jeanmarie." He stopped for breath and to jog his memory.

"How far down did the last ice go? How far down to the end?"

"Some late sheets extended as far south as the Ohio and Missouri rivers. Nearly to St. Louis."

"Now *that* will make Florida pretty damned cold. I used to live in Florida; I may go back there."

"Pleistocene men huddled in the tropics."

"*I* don't like the tropics; the tropics are filled with bugs and bats and things. Perhaps I'll go to Mexico with Harley, his wife is down there. Perhaps I'll go home with him—if she'll let me in." His gaze swung to the knitting and away again. "Did that old history mention ice falls? That old book which just came in?"

"Yes, among other things."

Fisher Highsmith searched her lap and then looked under the bucket seat.

Jeanmarie shook her head.

"There wasn't time to bring it along, but I read several pages while it was being reproduced." Jeanmarie neglected to add that she had also memorized those pages; a statement was unnecessary. Competent polylibrarians committed to memory everything read, seen, heard, and experienced by them and retained the data for future need.

"Tell me."

"A fall of stones and small ice balls was recorded at Truro, Cornwall, in April 1821. Another like fall was noted at Clairvaux, France, in August 1842. The ice was mixed with mud and an unidentified substance resembling chicle. The historian referred to it as a rubbery substance but did not otherwise describe it."

Dubiously: "Hail or sleet."

"It may have been." She was noncommittal.

"A rubbery substance, chicle."

"So it was reported."

"Who was the historian? What was his name?"

"Charles Fort."

"Never heard of him."

She made no reply.

Fisher Highsmith propped his chin in the open palm

of his hand and gently rocked in the bucket seat. The feathery trembling of the aircraft that had been sensed on the ground was absent now, and there were only the ever-present gusts of gale winds which sometimes struck the craft and teetered it.

After a while he turned back to the woman.

"Jeanmarie, was there any evidence of glaciation that long ago? In 1842? Can we build a correlation between ice and debris? Ice sheets and mud bricks?"

She paged through her memory. "I don't think so. The winters were more severe in Europe and North America during that century; there is a large body of information on heavier snowfalls and generally lower temperatures, but the condition did not persist and the intervening summers were quite hot. During that time the major glaciers moved less than four meters per year. I don't sense a historical connection."

"I thought I was discovering something."

"Don't rule out that possibility."

Highsmith looked his next question.

"Eisely said that catastrophe breeds discovery. He had observed that significant changes may occur in a time of catastrophe; he believed that early man discovered and first used fire during the previous glaciation, that primitive man moved out of the tropics and followed the melting ice sheets northward carrying fire with him. Supporting evidence to that theory was found in Asian caves about a century ago. The theory seems to be valid."

"Who was Eiseley?"

"A twentieth-century naturalist."

"A recon man?"

"Only in a sense. Not literally, not like you."

"I wonder what I've discovered," Fisher mused. "My head persists in trying to build a correlation; it wants me to find or fabricate a link between the ice and the debris, one and the other. My head hurts."

"Keep trying," she urged him.

"Fish, frogs, sticks, and stones. I don't have any fish or frogs yet but I suppose I can look forward to them. And the chicle, let's not forget the chicle. I've got a double handful of shards of something—it isn't rubber and it isn't plastic but maybe the chicle will stick it all together. And I've got *bricks*. Somebody must be turning out bricks by the hundreds or the thousands, year in and year out. You'd think he would get tired."

"Or she."

"She?"

"Both sexes were employed in brickmaking in ancient times."

"It's a damn tedious job."

"Slaves had little choice."

"Well, they aren't slaves today and it's *still* a damned tedious job."

Harley asked: "Who makes mud bricks?"

"The peasants in Pan-Arabia, that's who. They're still at it, making them in the same old way their ancestors did in Iraq centuries ago, and in Mesopotamia thousands of years ago. Nothing has changed—not anything. The geography and the politics and the peasants and the bricks are the same. You'd think *they* would get tired."

"Did the agency investigate that? Did the agency question those peasants?"

Highsmith looked at the doctor and said solemnly: "They wouldn't speak to us, Harley. They're mad at us because of that Egyptian squabble; our government backed the wrong politician." And when the doctor attempted to rise from his seat to stare at him, Highsmith waved an imaginary flag—a little flag twirled between thumb and forefinger.

Harley deliberately turned his back—or tried to—and busied himself by looking out of the window.

Jeanmarie was puzzled. "I don't perceive a joke."

"My jokes are too subtle for mortal understanding," Fisher Highsmith told her.

"But our government was not involved in the recent Egyptian matter. It couldn't afford to get involved."

"Jeanmarie, you have brown eyes. Are you married?"

She seemed taken aback, and then said: "No."

"Bully. I'm mad about brown-eyed unmarried women." He studied the eyes for a thoughtful moment and then added: "I'm not married either. Isn't that a coincidence?"

The pilot interrupted. *I'm* not married."

"Jump out of the aircraft," Highsmith retorted.

Highsmith was saying: "I can sympathize with those oldtimers, those people in 1821 or 1842 or whatever. If it can't be explained, throw it away and pretend it never fell. Or blame it on a passing aircraft—pilots are always dropping things out of their pockets."

"There were no aircraft in 1821 or 1842, with the possible exception of hot-air balloonists."

"Well, then, blame it on an earthquake."

Jeanmarie said quietly: "That was done, once."

"The hell it was!"

The pilot broke in once more. "Will you shut up and let her tell it? I want to hear about it."

Highsmith affected surprise. "I thought you bailed out back there?"

"The earthquake—the earthquake!"

Jeanmarie stopped the squabbling.

"A fall of heated stones occurred at Charleston, South Carolina, in Setember 1886, about four days after a severe earthquake. Some authorities in the city made an attempt to blame the fall on the earthquake, but they were unable to explain precisely how it was responsible. The historian tended to belittle them."

"Is that all? Nothing more?"

"Nothing more was reported."

"Heated stones," Highsmith repeated. "Heated by what? Didn't anyone follow that up?"

"Nineteenth-century governments had no investigative programs similar to ours. The incident was mentioned briefly in the local newspapers and then ignored until the historian reported it at a later date."

Highsmith twisted around in his seat, stretching the lap belt. "Heated stones, Harley. Some of those bodies were burned."

"*Not* by stones or earthquakes," Harley retorted.

"By what, then?"

"If I said they were radiation burns, you'd think of spacers again."

"No, I wouldn't. I promise."

"*I* think they were radiation burns, some of the *other* doctors who performed autopsies think they were radiation burns, and we're *all* agreed those bodies didn't fall from the orbital platforms or imaginary saucers." Harley jabbed the needles in emphasis. "That's fantastic."

"Nuclear-reactor accidents?" Highsmith questioned. "Ground accidents—those nuclear generating stations? Seawater converters? The ocean-farming stations? That new installation at Sandusky rehabilitating Lake Erie?"

"No, none of those. If an accident had happened in any of those places the corpses would have been shot through with radiation, and they *wouldn't* be found in Alberta or Saskatchewan. No, not that."

Facetiously: "Steaming stones? Hot rocks?"

A solemn reply. "I had considered weapons."

Fisher Highsmith betrayed his astonishment.

Harley said: "If you can build brick spaceships, I can think radiation weapons. I can!"

"I was just joking, Harley. See my flag?"

"I wasn't," the doctor declared. "The burns on those other bodies weren't caused by heated stones or burning oil, they weren't turned over a spit, they didn't tumble through a fire. I know a radiation burn when I see one."

Highsmith gestured helplessly. "There's no radiation up here, except maybe for the sergeant's gear and the stuff in the kitchen—the oven and things."

"Just so. What are you going to do about it?"

Highsmith looked at him for a time, then answered: "I'm working on the problem."

"Good luck. A fresh one has just come down."

Fisher Highsmith swung back to the small window at his shoulder and again searched the horizon for ice scarps, but found his vision blunted. The sky was black with cloud, the brilliant moon lost behind, and he realized they had flown in under the permanent cloud cover. Their craft was nearing Lloydminster. Frost framed the outer edges of the glass where those edges fitted into the chill skin of the fuselage, but now the window showed him only the aircraft's outboard running lights. Winds were gusty.

"The moon is gone."

A noncommittal grunt from the pilot was the only answer. Silence grew in the cabin.

Highsmith thought now of weapons, and of battlements, and wondered why he'd overlooked those possibilities before. He'd spent all his time attempting domestic reconstructions, kitchen works, household artifacts, with nary a thought to weaponry and battlements. Had he been wasting his time? He'd tried to build a hearth, a firewall, a chimney, an oven, an altar, a door stoop, but none had worked for him. The mud bricks had refused to cooperate. There was a sense of rightness and wrongness to reconstruction and he'd known that everything attempted was wrong before it was half done.

He had never considered the possibility of warfare but now he began rearranging old patterns in his mind, fitting his supply of bricks into first one shape and then another, jogging them, reshuffling them, mentally building mud ramparts and bastions, parapets and embrasures, searching for that one significant line which would supply an image for the whole. Some one clue, no matter how small. He recognized the probability that his debris did not represent an entire artifact, an entire building, whatever that building may have been; he accepted the working supposition that the hundreds of bricks and pieces of bricks recovered from the many falls represented only a section of something—or sections of several somethings—but the elusive somethings puzzled and frustrated him. The many broken pieces had been carefully cemented together to form bricks and almost-bricks, and the results had in turn been fitted together in attempts to form a supporting wall, an altar, an oven . . . They would not work.

The best he had managed was a shallow corner where two stunted walls joined. That was a mockery. He'd torn down those poor walls and attempted a second and a third formation, but each time ended with a shallow corner.

A careful scrutiny of each brick revealed how it had been used and how it *should* be used in reconstruction. *This* one was an interior brick in the wall, with others like it pressing against it from above and below, others like it pressing against it at either end, and with the two narrow sides exposed to the weather. *This* brick was a bottom-layer brick, a foundation piece, laid end to end with it's companions and admitting to no other use or position. *This* was a top-layer brick revealing a contact only on its underside and at each end; and finally *this* was an end piece where the—whatever it was, whatever it had been—abruptly stopped. Broken pieces often fitted into this hole or that hole, but other broken pieces would fit nowhere and he laid them aside on the assumption they belonged to other bricks not yet recovered.

Bottom-layer bricks were the easiest to identify: weeds, grass, twigs, and sometimes small stones were embedded in their flattened undersides. The agency lab at Billings had identified the weed as chickweed and the grass as common rye grass of a temperate zone; both were relatively fresh and that was an added puzzle. The pebbles were simply glacial gravel.

Top-layer bricks had been exposed to weathering, to sun and moisture, over a prolonged period, and they sometimes tended to chip and crumble when handled roughly. Nothing had rested on them, as would rest on a foundation wall; neither roof beam nor lodgepole nor thatched covering—they had remained exposed to the weather for all of their useful life. Highsmith *had* made one small discovery, an exciting find. One brick had revealed the imprint of bird feet and a dropping where the bird had rested briefly while the brick was moist.

End bricks were simply end bricks, with the one end exposed to the same weathering and the opposite butted to a companion. Interior bricks readily revealed they had served as interior pieces with their sides exposed to the weather; a visual examination revealed their flattened planes and a micrometer gave evidence of the weight that had pressed down upon them, particularly those near the bottom of the heap. Some bricks appeared to be older than others and were constructed with a sand mix; they didn't wear as well as later ones made only with mud, or sometimes mud and clay. But old or new, they wouldn't work for him.

The best he had managed was that shallow corner where two walls joined, and he was ashamed of *that*.

Each of those walls was less than a meter in height, and just over a meter in linear length: a dwarf wall that had originally been built in open country on grassland —in a temperate zone—having no protective cover or roof to fend off the rain, and supporting nothing other than a small bird which had stopped there briefly. It hadn't been a load-bearing wall and the only thing it reminded him of now, after the doctor's suggestion, was a child's snow fort. A snow fort under sunny skies.

It made a poor ravelin.

He twisted around to face the doctor. "Harley, it made the sorriest ravelin you ever saw."

Jeanmarie was quick to catch his meaning as always.

Harley demanded: "What ravelin? Where?"

Jeanmarie offered: "A ravelin is a small defensive work, a temporary structure or shield having only two faces running to a point to form a salient angle. It is temporary in that it cannot be defended for long; it loses its value as a defensive work when the opposing side completes a flanking movement or approaches from the rear. A ravelin is intended only to blunt frontal assaults, and to gain additional time for the forces defending the main position, as in a fort or castle."

The doctor's expression did not change; a mental image had failed to form in his mind.

"Harley—that short, stunted brick wall I put together in the shop. Remember it?"

"I remember it. I do! And I remember your swearing when you tore it apart and tried to put it together in another way. You don't have an imaginative vocabulary, Fisherman. You don't."

"It will improve around you," Highsmith promised. "But *that*'s a ravelin, if you're willing to stretch a very large point, if you can imagine *that* one being defended by children or midgets. It's too low and too short. An enemy could jump it."

"Someone must have built them."

"A ravelin isn't worth a damn after the enemy circles about and comes in on you from the side, either side, but they were used in . . . in . . ." He turned to the woman.

She said: "Most often in the sixteenth and seventeenth centuries, to provide a defense in depth for the fortress behind them. They were forerunners of the pillbox and the Egyptian bikpost. They were of a height and width to conceal two men, and usually a number of them were widely scattered over the approaches to the fortress, although some military engineers preferred to erect them around the drawbridge. The troops manning the ravelins could safely withdraw into the fortress only if they were stationed near the drawbridge."

"And those out on the field were thrown away?"

"Yes, unless they lived to run."

"A stupid waste of manpower," Harley declared. "I wonder if our sixteen men were thrown away like that. The sixteen bodies our teams have picked up."

"Ah—we're back to the lost battle again."

"I don't understand," Jeanmarie said.

"You missed that part, you missed the good part—you were out of the room," Highsmith told her. "Harley said our dead men are coming in like stragglers from a lost battle, like flotsam from an unknown earthquake."

"An unknown disaster," Harley muttered. "Disaster."

"Same thing. Harley, none of those sixteen men could have used my ravelin—if it *is* a ravelin. They would have stuck up in the air like standing targets, head and shoulders exposed. I'd like to read those autopsy reports. Did you do any autopsies?"

"Two of them."

"Were those two about as tall as Jeanmarie?"

"About that. Yes, about that."

"Jeanmarie couldn't hide behind my ravelin."

"I disagree. She could hide."

"But you saw the reconstruction!"

"Fisherman, I didn't say she could stand and fight behind it; I *didn't*. I said she could hide behind it and that is a different matter, don't you see? She would be wholly concealed on her back, on her side, on her stomach, on her knees. She could *hide* behind it."

"Did those lost warriors fight on their backs, their sides, their stomachs, or on their knees?"

Harley passed over the sarcasm. "Were those men fighting or hiding when they fell down on us?"

Highsmith opened his mouth to retort, and then closed it. He looked at the doctor and finally said: "I don't know. I don't know what they were doing."

Jeanmarie asked: "Are you accepting the warrior theory? Are you accepting a defensive work?"

"I don't know that either. I'll work on the problem."

Harley said: "Everyone has problems. My wife's cousin has problems. Go talk to him."

"I didn't know your wife had a cousin; I didn't know you had a wife until an hour ago. What problem?"

"Retarded dolphins."

Fisher Highsmith pursed his lips and studied the man. "Are you waving a little flag?"

"I am not. My wife's cousin is with the Navy at Key West; he is a marine psychologist working with the dolphins at Key West. This is top secret; no one is supposed to repeat it." Harley stopped knitting to waggle a cautionary finger. "The dolphins are being trained to slip into Havana harbor and do something, I don't know what; her cousin won't talk about *that*. The government is still trying to topple the Cuban People's Republic, and the dolphins are supposed to do something. They are.

. . . .

"My wife's cousin sends them off on their missions quite healthy and happy and filled with patriotism, but they fail—they come back disturbed, upset, mentally ill. Some of them don't come back at all, some of them are found wandering around in the Gulf Stream, disoriented. Lost dolphins. Retarded dolphins. A problem."

"I heard about that," the pilot volunteered.

"I read a paper on the subject," Jeanmarie said. "It is believed the dolphins collide with submarine nets in the harbor and are electrically or chemically stunned. Dead fish have been observed floating on the surface near the nets whose locations are known. Research is going forward on the matter."

"Everyone knows our secrets," Harley complained.

"I don't," Highsmith reassured him. "And I won't say a word about this, not a word, and you tell your wife's cousin to keep quiet about Jeanmarie's paper. It may be confidential." He transferred his attention to the girl. "I think I'll work on ravelins, I *like* the idea of ravelins, I'm going to build more ravelins."

"Fill the shop with ravelins; fill it!" the doctor said without humor. "Build them in the tower, the commissary, the repair shops, the kitchen, the dorm—*your* end of the dorm. Stay away from my end, my bed. Jeanmarie can speak for herself. We'll make straw men to stack behind the ravelins, stretch them out on their straw bellies. I may even lend you a corpse; I may do that."

"But, Harley, you gave me the idea!"

"I'm sorry."

"I still want to read those autopsy reports," the recon man said. "Jeanmarie, will you get them for me?"

"Yes, sir."

"Why?" the doctor demanded.

Facetiously: "If the warriors fought on their knees they will have calluses; if they hid on their bellies they will have grass or mud in their teeth—in their mouths. I want to know about that."

"Some of them had mud in their mouths," the doctor retorted. "A natural thing, considering. And some had traces of water in their throats and lungs. Moisture."

"There you are! You see? I was right!" Highsmith paused at a sobering second thought and stared at the doctor. "Were they swimming?"

"Certainly not, of course not. They died in the mud

or in the snow; they ate mud or inhaled snow as they died violent deaths. That's a natural thing, considering."

Slowly, incredulously: "Harley—Harley, if you found snow or water in their throats and lungs, that means they died *here* in the snowfields."

"Not necessarily, not at all. It may have been snowing there, wherever *there* is, wherever they had lived." The doctor hesitated and fell to studying the garment in his lap. After a while he said: "I won't make a definite statement, I won't. I can't say where they died. I know only that mud or snow was present at the scene."

"But not a river? A lake? A drowning?"

"No, none of those. The lungs would have been filled and the skin would have revealed an immersion."

"Harley, I wonder if—"

The pilot yelled at him, cutting off the thought. The pilot was twisted around in his seat belt, pointing to a set of earphones affixed to the fuselage above the seat. He tapped his own phone in signal. Highsmith fitted the set over his head and adjusted the mouthpiece.

"Highsmith here."

"Fisherman, this is Busby on Search Three. Are you bringing the doctor with you?"

"Yes—of course."

"Then hurry, dammit! This man is alive."

"What?"

"I said old Seventeen is alive; we can see movement in the sack—the thermal sack. But it won't do him or you any good if you're walking—somebody beat the hell out of him. We thought he was dead."

Highsmith leaned forward to the limit of his belt and thumped the pilot on his back with a balled fist.

"You heard him—jump, move! They've got a live corpse out there, one that's still breathing. *Go!*"

The doctor was so startled he dropped his knitting, and then could not bend to recover it because of the acceleration.

FOUR

Iron

The boatman went in under cover of night, paddling soundlessly toward the many fires burning on shore. The soft wind blowing across the water carried no immediate danger but yet he moved cautiously, aware that it was not wholly favorable to him.

He had discovered the intruders by daylight, long before the sun had set. The noise of their coming hadn't carried to him because he was a great distance across the inland sea, and that same distance refused to give him a scent, but his eyesight was sharp enough to find them. They were a troop. They had erupted onto the plains in great number, spilling out of the shallow valley lying between two rangy hills and running down to the waterline to play in the icy waters of the sea. It made him think of thirsty animals, but they did not drink as animals and seemed content to dabble in it, taste it, throw it at one another. There were so many of them that when the first few reached the waterline, others were still coming out of the valley behind and marching at a leisurely pace.

Never in all his life had he seen that many people together in one place. It was an astonishing sight.

He hid from them.

The boatmaker dared not go down to his boat during the daylight hours, dared not move along the beach for fear they would find him as easily as he'd seen them; he kept to the high grasses and the sparse timber growing on his side of the water while he waited for darkness. The soft summer wind continued to blow up through the valleys from the south, blowing their sounds and scents

away from him and out across the inland sea. Many
times during the long wait for nightfall he saw fish leaping in the water near his boat, and once a fat watersnake
skimmed the surface in search of prey, but he didn't
break cover to go in chase; he was sure the invaders
would discover him. He stayed hungry.

At dusk the newcomers built fires along the distant
shore, and he was again astonished. There were no trees
on that side of the sea—no driftwood along those
shores; the only timber near at hand was here, on this
side, and he stayed here because some of the trees were
of a size and a quality for building, some of them made
seaworthy boats when they were properly cut and hollowed, and the best of them remained serviceable for a
very long time—for more than one or two summers
when fish and game returned. But the newcomers built
fires; they carried wood with them.

By that he knew they had traveled a very long way, a
tiring distance; there were many forests to the south beyond the ranging hills but the nearest treeline was so distant it was beyond his means to cut and transport a single tree or boat from there to this water. An impossible
task. The invaders had traveled a great distance, and
large numbers of them had packed in wood for the fires.

They burned brightly at nightfall.

The boatman crept down to the shore and studied the
water, looking for but not finding a reflection of the sky;
sometimes the water stayed bright long after the sun had
set and a searching man could see a very long distance
over it; sometimes high clouds caught up the light of the
hidden sun and threw it down on the water. He rolled
over on his back to search the sky. There would be no
moon—the moon had been away for many nights, and
he knew from experience when and where it would
come back again. Two bright stars, sky brothers almost
touching, hung in the high north above the distant, unseen ice wall; he used those brothers for direction and
guidance when traveling at night, for unlike the moon
they were always there, always together in the same
place.

When he was satisfied, when he had scanned the sea and tested the wind for sound or scent of another, he put his tools into the boat and pushed off. To leave anything behind was folly; another man would steal his tools.

He owned two hand axes, one better than the other because it was fashioned from the thighbone of a great hulking animal that had no name; he'd seen such an animal only once and had stalked it for two days before bringing it down. The many prongs on the animal's head had been useful for digging and scraping but the thighbone had been a treasure. The other hand ax was made from chipped stone and was useful in its way, but he favored the first. He possessed two round, flat throwing stones fastened together with a braided grass rope reinforced by leather strips taken from that same great animal; he'd seen other men using the stones, and only recently had discovered they were much more reliable when reinforced with leather. Braided grass rope often broke when the game fought back, letting the animals go free. And finally he had a handful of bone knives for infighting and for skinning game; they broke easily and he didn't place too much reliance on them. He always searched for a better knife.

He was downwind of them, near their shore. Smoke and fumes from their fires easily carried to him now and he slowed his pace, paddling slowly toward the beach. A new scent was mixed with the fires, a pungent and strangely exciting scent so heavy on the wind that he assigned it to the people there. He knew them to be strangers.

The prow of the boat suddenly touched bottom, and he climbed out into the icy water to swing it about and beach it with the blunt stern resting on the pebbly sand. The maneuver caused a small grating sound and he froze beside the craft waiting to see if he was discovered. Nothing. The boat was well away from the light of the nearest fires.

The boatman gathered up a few tools and darted

away into the grass beyond the waterline, a fleeting shadow in the night. He ran soundlessly on bare feet. The intent was to circle the camp, to come back in on it about the middle, far from his boat but yet in a position where the wind would continue to favor him. The fires on the shore were beacons and the heavy smells on the night wind guided him. When he reached a position that satisfied him, he stopped running and began the approach. The camp was so vast and the people so many that it and they stretched away to the south, away from the inland sea, reaching back to the middle of the great plain lying between the sea and the hills. He realized quickly that he was not in the center of it at all, but still at the northern end where that end circled down to the water. He hesitated, looking down at it and then back to the dark place where his boat rested. Caution dictated that he go no deeper into the great plain. The wary approach continued.

The boatman nearly stumbled over a rope of something knee-high in the grass.

He dropped to his belly in an instinctive action and crawled under the obstacle, turning to look up at it. This was a strange thing, a new thing, a rope not fashioned of braided grass nor one made of leather strips, but yet it was solid and taut and had a peculiar odor. It was held above the ground by poles, and when he turned his head he could see the rope and poles stretching away in the darkness to either side of him. A barrier; a guardian line around the camp. The boatman put out a cautious finger to touch it, and at once was stung by an enormous shock. He nearly cried out in the night, betraying himself, and fell back in the concealing grass to nurse his hand and arm because the shock had leaped through his finger and gone to the shoulder. It had been a painful torment.

A frightening thing happened next.

Behind him, over his head and behind him in the camp, a great blinding light burned away the darkness —a light more brilliant than the brightest moon he'd ever known, a moving light that stabbed out into the night and searched along the length of rope. The light moved and probed. He could clearly see the taut rope above him and the poles to either side as the blinding brilliance swept by. The boatman hugged the ground, not daring to move or breathe. It passed over his position without seeing him, and he felt a great surging relief as it swept on down the length of stinging rope in search of an intruder. When it was gone he climbed to his knees in the enveloping darkness and crawled away, hurrying because he suspected it might come again. The light penetrated to the far end of the camp, hesitated there, and began a return sweep along the ropeline. The boatman watched in open-mouthed wonder as the radiance crept toward him—toward the place where he had lain—and quickly threw himself flat as it neared.

The blinding thing followed the ropeline all the way to the beach and played on the water for a time, then went out as suddenly as it had started burning. He held his position, waiting for it to come again, but the night stayed dark. After a while he gathered up his courage and his tools and prowled forward, alert for any other obstacle in his way. The scent was stronger and nearby.

Because he was forewarned and moving cautiously, he found the new pole first and *then* the second line of defense affixed to it. The ropeline was close to the ground, about the height of a man's foot, and hidden in the grass to trip the unwary. He studied the pole carefully but found no other lines fastened to it, and then with a new impudence stepped over the tripper and went in.

Something moved near at hand.

The boatman sank to his knees and spread his tools on the ground before him, arranging them in a semicircle at his fingertips. He lifted his head to smell the air.

The sentry was downwind of him, coming forward.

The boatman's fingers curled around his ax handle as he waited for the prowling figure to discover him. He didn't understand why the other had failed to catch his scent, had failed to see him crouching there in the grass; the new people must be poor hunters. The sentry idled along, picking a casual way alongside the concealed ropeline but yet far enough away to avoid stepping on it. There was no pretense of stealth or vigilant patrolling; the sentry appeared to rely on the ropeline as invincible. The new people were poor warders.

Another few steps brought the silhouetted figure between the boatman and the fires down on the beach, a clear and inviting target. The sentry paused to search the sky overhead and the plains beyond the ropeline, and then turned to look down on the fires. People were singing there. The boatman was thunderstruck at the lack of caution.

His fingers left the ax handle and darted to the throwing stones. He rose to his knees at the sentry's back and began whirling one of the stones above his head, allowing the braided rope to inch through his fingers until the stone was flying in a high wide arc above him. The gathering speed of the missile raised a whisper in the air. The sentry sensed the new sound above the singing and began a turn. The boatman opened his fingers and let fly.

It caught the standing target around the neck.

The boatman leaped from concealment, racing after his crude bolas. He found the sentry on sagging legs, jerking, gasping for breath and tearing frenziedly at the braided rope wound around the neck; a strangling sound rose from the tortured throat and sought escape through the open mouth. The boatman smashed a heavy fist into the mouth and quickly struck a second time, a hammerheavy blow onto the side of the jaw. The sentry toppled, and the boatman followed the body down to hide in the high grass.

No outcry.

The heady scent was overpowering. He was astonished again—in a day of astonishments—to discover the sentry fully clothed in some strange covering that reached from head to foot; even the arms and legs were protected by the artificial wrapping while the feet were encased in soft fashioned-leather hulls or pods. He ran his hands over the body in growing wonder, surprised at what his fingers were finding, and then turned the body over on its back to look into the face. A woman's face. He put an exploratory hand to the breasts, following their contours and knowing the truth of discovery. In the following moment he found the wondrous knife at her waist and pulled it from its sheath to marvel: the long blade was polished and gleaming, and actually seemed to reflect the dim light of the fires when he held it up to stare at it.

He tried to pull away the belting at the waist to recover he sheath, but could not puzzle out the fastener in the middle. His new knife cut the sheath free. The keen edge of the blade was another surprise and in his ignorance he actually cut through the artificial covering under the sheath and punctured the skin. Once more his hands roamed over the inert body in search of any other treasure to take with him, but he found nothing more than a talisman dangling from the woman's throat. He wouldn't touch that; it was courting trouble to take another's magic piece.

A dark, almost colorless object lay on the ground under one crooked leg, a small but bulky thing having a handle on one side. The boatman picked it up, smelled it, looked into the hole at one end, and put it down again. It was useless to him and he had the treasure he wanted.

He lifted the sentry's head and unwound the braided rope from about her neck, then crawled away from the body to recover his good ax. Moving carefully, he located the inner pole and stepped over the tripper with caution. Free of the inner defense, he trotted away into the night. The outer line was hurtled with a running leap.

They had found his boat. Three of the strange people were on the beach, standing at the stern of his boat.

The boatman knew that a momentary advantage was his and he didn't hesitate. The three were standing with their backs to him and he had already learned their fatal inability to detect his scent. He ran down onto the beach on bare feet and hurled his good ax at the nearest, aiming for the head. It split the skull, nearly tearing the head from the trunk, and the body toppled forward onto the stern of the boat. The others jumped, gawked down at the bloody thing, and attempted a tardy recovery. They were turning.

The boatman hurled his throwing rocks. There was no time to swing them, to race one around his head and fire it at the enemy—there was barely time to aim and throw and he slung them with all his strength. A rock caught one of the figures, knocking it off balance and back into the water; the other rock went wide of its mark but the rope belted the third across the chest, staggering it. Somebody cried out, a cry that was half a scream—a woman's scream—and he knew these three were like the sentry behind him.

The boatman raced in to the woman who was struggling with his rope and rammed his new knife into her stomach, plunging in high just below the rib cage. He didn't wait to see her fall but turned on the other sitting in the water and aimed a brutal kick at her face. She dodged it, rolling away in the cold water and then struggling to regain her feet. He heard a shrill, piercing whistle.

The blinding light blazed up in the camp.

The boatman hastily rolled the body off the stern of his boat and pushed off, running out into the water to gain speed. The good ax was left behind. He was afraid of that brilliant white fire, afraid that it would touch him, and the only safety he knew was the open sea. The boat sped away from the blood-strewn beach. He paddled with long, powerful strokes, not caring now about the noise.

The moving light touched the beach, lingered on the gory tableau there, and then began a sweep across the water. It picked up the boat's wake. The boatman saw it coming from the corner of his eye and dropped to the bottom to hide, knowing security in the stout wooden sides of the craft. The light didn't burn things: the stinging rope and the poles and the grass had not flashed into flame. It seemed a little less bright here, less blinding than it had been back there at the defense line, and he began to doubt that it could follow him all the way across the icy water to his own shore.

He clutched his new knife to his chest and waited.

FIVE

Ice

Old Route Five, the Fort Battleford road, was lost somewhere beneath the snows, and the ice loomed behind it. The ice was massive and malignant, an enormous landberg.

Fisher Highsmith was unable to move.

He stood helpless, vulnerable, rooted in tormented fear. A cold wind washed down the rugged slope of ice and bathed him with chill malevolence. The great escarpment loomed over him, above and beyond him, dwarfing him—a stupendous creeping mountain of frozen fresh-water seas; it threatened him, threatened his reason and sanity and well-being and threatened death if he hesitated, yet he could not move. The frigid mountain seemed ready to engulf him. The wind was its frozen breath, piercing his garments and plucking at his bones. Highsmith couldn't see the top of it; the top was lost in blackness and he was not aware of the invisible line between ice and sky.

News pictures had not adequately prepared him for this enormity of ice, and now it frightened him. This was the leading edge of the new glaciation, but only the edge, and he tried to imagine the bulk behind it.

The doctor followed him out of the aircraft.

Harley jumped down into snow above his waist and promptly fell, thrashing about with flailing arms until he found the lower edge of Highsmith's parka and managed to right himself. He pulled himself out of the snow by clawing up the gaunt frame of Highsmith, and then glared at the recon man because he'd been offered no help. The younger man was staring at the ice. The doctor pushed past him with a muttered impatience and struggled toward a flaring beacon, wanting to meet the search party. He'd already seen the ice at Egg River and Cameron Bay, and now he spared it no more than a troubled glance.

Jeanmarie and the pilot stayed in the aircraft. Their faces were flattened against the frosty windows, staring up fixedly at the monstrous landberg.

Highsmith couldn't guess at its height because the top remained hidden from him; he made no attempt to guess the mass and volume because of the insanity of the idea. It was huge, frigid, and frightening, moving toward him at an implacable pace—his imagination told him it was visibly moving, rolling down on him where he stood, but reason fought to reject that fantasy; Jeanmarie had said it crept forward at only sixty-one meters per year and he could stand hip-deep in snow all night without seeing a perceptible movement. *Only* sixty-one meters per year: that was almost a record.

The bitter Arctic cold pierced his clothing and triggered an uncontrollable shivering; he had forgotten that he was disconnected from the aircraft heating unit.

Highsmith made an effort to tear his gaze away from the ice escarpment—it was as difficult as looking away from Medusa. He forced himself to turn and look at the lighted windows of the aircraft, at the mesmerized faces of Jeanmarie and the pilot. He continued the turn until he faced the beacons. They were brilliant yellowish suns in the falling snow.

The men of Search Three were struggling toward him with a heavy thermal sack slung between them: it was an awkward burden and caused them some difficulty. Harley had simply stopped in the snow and waited for the men and their load to reach him; it was too arduous to go forward. Unlike the men on the search team, none of the new arrivals had possessed the wits to bring snowshoes with them. The doctor waited until the burden had passed, then turned to follow it.

Fisher Highsmith stared morbidly at the sack as it went by, seeking some movement within it. An electric cord trailed through the snow; it had been plugged into a heat generator on the team's sled until a moment ago. The sight of that cord triggered another spasm of shivering and Highsmith remembered he was unplugged.

Someone thrust a few objects into his hand.

"Fisherman? Are you the Fisherman?"

"I'm the frozen Fisherman."

"Hello—I'm Busby. Your man is still alive, or was until a couple of minutes ago. Damnedest sight I ever saw! Hold on to these things—they came down with him." He had given Highsmith a broken bow, a knife, and a strange black object that was utterly foreign to him.

Highsmith stared at the curious object in his hand. It had a handle, and a cold rubbery feel to it.

"What is it?"

"How would I know? That's *your* job, old buddy; I've done mine. It bounced off a shelf up there somewhere and followed him down—it came down with that crazy slowness like everything else does: drifting, floating down. The bow was wrapped around his neck and the knife was in his hand—he had a death grip on it."

"Did you see him fall?"

"I *said* he tumbled down on our heads."

"But did you see him hit the ice shelf *first?* Did you see him come down from somewhere else and hit that shelf? Did he fall on you later?"

"Later, I guess. I think he came off the shelf."

"Did you go up on that shelf for a look around?"

"I'm not that crazy, Fisherman."

"How did he come down?"

"I've already said he fell on us."

"No, no, I don't mean that! Did he come down in a slow drift like the other debris, or did he come down hard?"

Busby paused in thought. "He came down hard. It

would have broken his back if he had hit bare ground."

"Ah—that's something."

"What?"

"I don't know, but it's something."

The thermal sack and its contents were stowed in the aircraft and now the men turned away, their job nearly done. The doctor scrambled inside after the body, calling to someone. Jeanmarie's face had already disappeared from the window and the pilot was sliding the door shut. The rescue was completed. The yellow beacons illuminated an expanse of trampled snow, a waiting sled, and the coated fuselage of the aircraft. Already it bore a thin white blanket. Seventeen was down and the many days of expectation were ended. It was the first live recovery.

Busby nudged him.

"Are you just going to stand there like some gawking tourist? Come on, Fisherman, move it—you're not plugged in, you'll freeze soon." He gestured toward the sled. "We're done here, we're flying back to Billings as soon as we reach camp. I know where there's a glow party going on and I've got an invitation. I'd invite you to come along, Fisherman, but you've got work to do now."

Busby turned and took a single step away.

"Where is Lloydminster?" Highsmith reached out quickly to stop him. "Where is the town?"

Busby turned him around to face north by northwest and pointed across his nose at the gigantic ice mass.

"In there. Under that, two kilometers or so." He peered at Highsmith in speculation. "You've got buck fever, old buddy, and if you don't know what that is ask your polylib. Now, go on—move it!" The group leader thumped him on the arm in parting and followed the last of his team over the snow to the sled.

Someone snuffed out a beacon and began dismantling it. Half-darkness gave the illusion of the glacier suddenly ballooning outward, threatening to topple over on the men working below it. The ice suddenly seemed alive. Behind Highsmith, the pilot yelled an unkind thing.

Highsmith pulled his fascinated gaze away from the ice Medusa and struggled to pull his freezing feet from the deep snows. His legs were numb as he climbed awkwardly into the cabin. He would have turned for a last look at the great landberg but the pilot gave him an unexpected assist inward and slammed the door shut.

There was no time to buckle in. The aircraft's abrupt vertical takeoff was an unsuccessful attempt at a compromise: the pilot's concern for the nearly dead man and his own fear of being trapped under a racing glacier. The same illusion had snared him.

"Easy!" Harley cried. "I said easy!"

"Easy it is, Doc."

"Call the agency. Don't bother with the office in Billings, call Washington South! Tell them what we have here, tell them what we found. I want a fresh supply of IV, I want a portable hospital unit, I want a couple of nurses. Fly everything in, *now*. Call them."

"Yessir, Doc."

"Tell them I demand priority."

"Yessir, I'm telling them."

"Make them acknowledge everything."

"Yessir." The aircraft straightened out on flight.

Highsmith put the weapons and the curious artifact in his bucket seat and dropped to his knees on the cabin floor beside Harley to see what the doctor was doing. The thermal sack had been opened to expose the head and torso, and Harley had scraped dirt from those areas where he now worked. A cardiogun rested on the floor between his knees.

Highsmith said: "The man needs a bath."

Seventeen appeared to be naked, as many of his dead predecessors had been, and was cast from the same mold: unkempt black hair that covered his forehead and ears and grew thickly down the back of his neck; he had a dark bushy beard, thick eyebrows, thick hair matted in his nostrils, and a smothering tangle of hair on his chest and arms. His skin was rough and beaten by sun and weather. The man had strong facial features and an even stronger body—in all, about one quintal of warrior or logger or manual laborer. An ancient knife scar began just below a missing earlobe and sliced down across his cheek to swollen, discolored lips. Those lips were open to reveal the strong white teeth of a carnivore.

Highsmith sucked in his breath as his examination traveled along the exposed portion of the body. The neck and shoulders were frostbitten, while his left arm and hand were frozen and already assuming a sickly black hue. His rib cage and his one good arm were bruised and bloodied, a silent testimony to the struggle that had knocked him down onto the ice shelf. Two new knife wounds lay beneath frozen trails of blood. He had been cut over the heart, and cut again from shoulder to elbow.

"I don't think he's had a bath since the day he was born." Highsmith's gaze moved along the arms. "Harley, look at his fingers! There's mud under the nails!"

"I've seen his fingers. He's going to lose them, as if that matters."

"If it *matters?* It *does* matter, doesn't it?"

"This arm must be amputated, don't you see, don't you see? The fingers aren't important now."

"But there's mud under his nails! My brickmaker!"

"I'll give you the fingers," the doctor snapped.

He removed a needle from a vein in the healthy arm, counted to thirty aloud, and pulled the trigger of the cardiogun now flattened against Seventeen's chest. The matted chest heaved in volcanic response and a growling rumble began climbing up the throat—a sound that failed just before it reached the swollen lips. The chest slumped.

Harley shouted at the pilot. "Did you call the agency? Did they acknowledge?"

"Yessir, Doc. It's coming, everything you want." He shot a glance at Highsmith and added: "Nurses."

"Off limits," Harley retorted. "No time for that."

Highsmith studied the frozen arm with a morbid fascination. "Look there, look at the mud on his arm—and on the left side of his face. Is it on his back too?"

"I haven't looked at his back."

"He rested on his left side behind the ravelin, in the mud—*if* he had a ravelin. I know he had the mud, he's filthy." Highsmith measured the length of the man with a practiced eye, a running assessment from shaggy head to the foot of the sack. "He *could* fit behind a ravelin lying down; he's less than a meter and a half tall. He *could* hide behind one, Harley. There's no snow or ice where he came from, no glaciation—he lived on the grasslands with mud and warm rains. His skin is tanned from the sun."

"It's covered with wounds, old and new."

"Well, yes, somebody *did* try to kill him."

"And where would that happy land be?"

"Almost anywhere in a temperate zone; right here in the United States of North America if we had a decent climate. That grass I found on the bricks was a common rye grass, a North American grass. *That* grass grew here before the ice."

"This fellow didn't grow here before the ice."

"I suppose not—but he lived in a warm climate. He couldn't very well run around naked in the snow and minus-sixty temperatures, not for long. A warm country."

Harley said: "I don't believe in teleportation."

Highsmith frowned at that, turning the unknown word end over end in his imagination without finding an answer. He looked at Jeanmarie. "Teleportation?"

She said: "Teleportation is the supposed art of traveling great distances by will power alone, not using a mechanical or natural means. A magic conveyance."

"Without an aircraft or a ship? Without walking?"

"Yes."

"I don't believe in magic," Highsmith agreed with the doctor. "This man didn't drift in from Mesopotamia or some such." He spent a long moment studying the man on the floor. "He owns a very good knife. Why didn't he cut his hair or trim his beard?"

"Primitive men don't often do that."

"He's primitive all right, but his knife isn't. I'll bet he stole that knife—slipped into a civilized town somewhere and stole it. A man who made mud bricks and built ravelins couldn't manufacture that knife."

"Let me see it," Jeanmarie asked.

Highsmith retrieved the knife and the broken bow from his seat and gave them to the woman. She studied each of the objects intently, paging through a mental catalogue in an attempt to identify and place each weapon in military history. Highsmith waited for her, holding his silence.

At last she said: "The bow is a Yakut type, a self-bow made of a single piece of wood. I think this wood is yew. It was commonly used in Siberia until the nineteenth century."

"Siberia!" Highsmith looked at the man on the floor. "But Siberia is also under ice; their glaciation is more extensive than ours."

Jeanmarie said: "I don't know the knife. I've never seen a weapon like it."

Highsmith was incredulous. "Not at all?"

"Not at all. The pattern and alloy are new to me."

The doctor said: "Give me that!" He took the knife from Jeanmarie and held it close to his glasses to examine the cutting edge. A moment later he was scrabbling through his medical kit, muttering under his breath.

"What are you going to do?" Highsmith asked.

"Amputate that arm, amputate it! Why didn't you tell me you had this knife?"

Fisher Highsmith looked at the doctor with dismay and deliberately pivoted on his knees, putting his back to the scene. The pilot was staring at *him*. After a moment he peeked over his shoulder to ascertain the reason for the silence behind him and found the doctor dipping the knife into a bottle of colorless solution. Jeanmarie was coolly watching the preliminaries. Highsmith swiveled back to the curious pilot and they locked glances.

Someone behind him sighed deeply once, but Highsmith could not say which of the three was responsible.

"What color are his eyes?" Highsmith asked afterward. "Have you looked?"

Harley said: "Blue."

The operation was complete and the stump sealed over at the shoulder in a thin plastic bandage that stretched like rubber to protect the joint and remaining tissue. Harley had cleaned the knife, studied it once more with open admiration, and handed it back to Highsmith. The aircraft cabin held a pungent tang associated with hospitals.

"Blue eyes—a blue-eyed warrior," Highsmith said soberly. He might have dropped down out of the Stone Age, fallen right out of yesterday onto the ice shelf today."

"I doubt it," the doctor retorted.

"He didn't tumble in here from Siberia," Highsmith insisted. "There may be blue-eyed warriors there, and they still may be using those crude bows, but he didn't drop in from Siberia yesterday *or* today. They don't make mud bricks, they don't build with mud bricks, they don't possess knives Jeanmarie has never seen before, and they don't have teleportation. All they have now is ice."

"I bitterly regret having mentioned a battle."

"I don't, Harley." Highsmith moved in on his knees near the patient. "Consider this man: we agree that he didn't live here before the ice, eight or ten or twelve thousand years ago. He didn't come from another land by magic, neither Siberia nor Mesopotamia; and he didn't fall down on us from an orbital platform or from a spacer."

Dryly: "We *do* agree on that."

Highsmith said: "I know one explanation. One."

"I'm waiting on it."

"The next age," Highsmith said. "He lived here *after* the ice."

The doctor peered at him and then looked around the cabin. "Did you bring that bourbon along?"

"No bourbon. I'm serious."

Heavy sarcasm: "The next age? Twenty-nine million years?"

"Of course not! Not *that* long."

"Only a million or so? A mere million?"

"Jeanmarie said that the glaciation comes and goes at

intervals; each time it covers only parts of the continent and then retreats." Highsmith flapped his hands. "Back and forth, every eight or ten or twelve thousand years like clockwork."

"I didn't say that!" she protested.

"Oh, please—let's not start that again. Give me a figure."

"There have been four major glacial advances in the past three hundred thousand years, plus several minor stages, of course. *Not* including the present one; it is too early to determine if this is a major or minor advance. If *this* glaciation does not endure beyond five thousand years and does not extend beyond the Great Lakes, it will be counted a minor advance. There were very many minor stages between the major periods of glaciation."

"Jeanmarie—please?"

"The last advance of ice anywhere, prior to this one, occurred only about eleven thousand years ago. A stage known as the Valders propelled an Ontario glacier down into southern Wisconsin and Michigan. It persisted about three thousand years and retreated eight thousand years ago."

"There!" Fisher Highsmith cried in triumph. "That's the figure. *That* one stayed around three thousand years."

"You'll still be an old man when this ice retreats."

"Harley, pay attention: if this man—if Seventeen didn't live in Saskatchewan earlier than the Valders, and doesn't live here today—*this* year, *this* ice,—then he has to live here tomorrow. He will live here *after* the ice retreats; three or four or five thousand years from now when the ice is gone. Seventeen is a temperate man, not an Arctic man. He migrated to Saskatchewan when it warmed up; he came in from somewhere else like Jeanmarie's man—ah, Eiseley's tropical man."

"I didn't see his flying machine out there."

Highsmith said: "Busby was afraid to climb up on the ice shelf. He didn't go topside at all."

"I didn't mean an aircraft, I didn't! I meant some

kind of machine to carry him through five thousand years!"

Highsmith hesitated. "Well, I'm working on—"

"*Don't* say it," Harley warned.

Highsmith fell silent and watched while the doctor again put the cardiogun to the thickly matted chest. Jeanmarie was slowly depressing the plunger on a needle inserted into the healthy arm. When the fluid had vanished from the glass, he made a signal to remove the needle and then began to counting aloud. They waited. When the count came to an end, Harley squeezed the trigger.

The body jerked in a single convulsion and the growling rumble began its second journey up the throat. Juglar veins bulged beneath the skin. Seventeen's mouth opened in readiness. The heavy rumble reached the lips and spilled out.

"Kilm!" Blurred sepulchral sound.

The doctor hurriedly closed the sack to the throat and turned up the thermostat. He left only the man's head and neck exposed, but kept a stethoscope tucked down inside the narrow opening. Seventeen was breathing noisily through his open mouth and moving his one arm in the sack.

Highsmith asked Jeanmarie: "Do you know that word?"

"No, but if it was English it may have been a contraction of 'Kill them.' "

"English!" He peered at the strong weathered face. "Can our brickmaking warrior be an Englishman? An American? A post-glacial American?"

"He could be any Caucasian."

"Up from the south," the doctor added dourly. "South Dakota."

"His arm—the other arm—is a recent freeze, isn't it, Harley? Say in the last few hours? It didn't happen a week or a month ago?"

"It's recent. This fellow was on that ice shelf longer than Busby knew; much longer."

"I thought so. Maybe he was moving around up there

and finally fell off, fell right down on them. Maybe he was hiding from *them*—from Search Three."

"Possibly. Likely."

"Those lights may have frightened him." Highsmith bent forward to study the old knife scar on the face. "But I want to know how he fell *down* on Search Three; how did he fall *down* from a warm world onto an ice shelf?"

Harley said testily: "He didn't fall so far; he didn't break his neck when he hit the ice and he didn't break it again when he tumbled into the snow."

"He *would* have if the snow hadn't made a cushion."

"But the ice, not the ice! No long fall there."

"Maybe there's a warm, sunny hillside a couple of meters above the glacier," Highsmith said facetiously. "Maybe he was sunning himself on a rock and slipped off." He had a sudden thought. "Harley—have you looked at his back yet? Is he *burned?*"

"I looked. It is."

"What kind of burn? Let me see!"

"No. Let him alone. I'm trying to keep him alive."

"But what kind of burn? What kind of weapon?"

Harley said: "I still think of radiation burns. The same kind of burn found on some of the others, and if you will show me a weapon capable of causing that kind of burn I will say to you, yes, that is the weapon that caused this type of burn. I will." He was short of patience.

Fisher Highsmith blinked at him with bemusement. Wordlessly, he reached over into his bucket seat for the nameless object and put it in the doctor's hand.

"What the devil is this?"

Highsmith kept silent, waiting on the doctor.

Jeanmarie said: "It is a curvilinear polygon with a handle on the apparent top side." She seemed to think that explanation enough.

"I didn't ask its shape, I can see the shape, I *do* have eyes! I asked what it was . . . is . . . "

Highsmith said: "Look at the short end."

The doctor turned it around by the handle and held

the object near his bifocals. The artifact was fashioned of an almost-black rubbery material and was about the size of a whole brick; it had a hefty, solid feel to it and weighed about half a kilogram; there were no visible seams and despite the relative warmth of the cabin it felt cold. Four fingers could be fitted snugly around the handle, leaving the thumb free. The smallest end of the polygon contained an opening vaguely like a muzzle, but then again it looked like the blunt spout of a water pitcher. There was no rifling within the muzzle, if it was a muzzle, nor was there a lip to catch the dripping if it was a pitcher.

"Don't pull the trigger, Harley. You're looking down the barrel."

The doctor fumbled in sudden alarm and would have dropped the artifact but for Highsmith's quick catch.

"It doesn't have a trigger, it doesn't!"

"No, but there has to be some way to fire it."

"Not in here!" the pilot cried with consternation. "Don't blow a hole in the cabin! We're almost home."

"I'll wait until we touch down and then blow a hole in the cabin," Highsmith assured him. He put the thing away, nestling it in the bucket seat with the knife and bow.

The doctor said doubtfully: "It might be some kind of a flashlight."

"That makes two of us with deficient imaginations, Harley. You'll never be a recon man." He looked to Jeanmarie. "Have you ever seen anything like it?"

"Only as an illustration."

He felt excitement. "An illustration of what?"

"Of a curvilinear polygon. It was one of several illustrations in an engineering handbook."

Highsmith let a silence grow between them.

The pilot twisted around to look at the group and to jab his finger at the deck beneath his feet. "Radio again. The sergeant's calling from the tower downstairs."

Highsmith put on the headset. "What's the good word, Sergeant?"

"Message just in from Search One, Fisherman." The communications man was talking with food in his mouth. "They're located in the northern sector of Regina, approaching the center of town. New debris falling."

"More of the damned stuff! The usual thing?"

"Well, yes and no. They're picking up gravel and pieces of wood, but this time they've found what appears to be part of a hollowed tree."

"A hollow tree? What is that—?"

"Wait, Fisherman, wait a minute. A *hollowed* tree. The trunk seems to have been hollowed out by an ax, or something like that. They don't have the whole tree; the fragment isn't very large, but there's enough of it to give you an idea."

"Anything else? Any kind of a weapon?"

"They haven't reported anything else."

"All right, Sergeant. Thanks. We're almost on top of you; we'll be home soon and I'll have a look at it."

The sergeant said, "Right, Fisherman. Out."

Highsmith hung up the headset and turned around. "Debris coming down in Regina. It'll be falling on the base next—mud bricks will be falling on the runway and things." He watched Seventeen struggling feebly in the sack, and sat down on the deck at the man's feet.

Impatiently: "That hollow tree!"

"Search One has picked up an old chunk of tree, a hollowed tree. Somebody hollowed it out with an ax."

Jeanmarie said quickly: "A dugout canoe."

"In downtown Regina? Or was the somebody using the canoe on the Waskana River—which is frozen over?"

"On Lake Agassiz," she replied. "It's *your* theory of the next interglacial period."

"Never heard of it," Fisher said. "And my theory is —" He came to a full stop, taken by surprise. "Oh, yes, I have! A prehistoric lake or inland sea."

"More properly, an inland sea. Lake Agassiz was formed when the Nelson, Warren, and Red rivers were blocked by the next-to-last glaciation stage. At its largest, the sea covered Manitoba and spilled over into Saskatchewan and Ontario. After that particular stage had retreated it drained off into Hudson Bay and expired, but a new sea was formed about eleven thousand years ago when the Valders glacier advanced from Ontario. The former shores of the second sea have been located by well-defined beaches it left behind, and there is reason to believe the *first* sea was equally large and covered the same area."

"Jeanmarie, if two advances created two seas in the same place, what is to prevent *this* ice from forming a third sea in just the same place?"

"I know of nothing to prevent it."

"Think of that," he marveled. "We may be sitting on the future shoreline of the *third* Lake Agassiz; our old base may be on the shore of a huge inland sea!"

"Or on the bottom of it."

Highsmith was startled at her suggestion. After a moment he said: "Men and bricks, sticks and stones and weapons, and now a piece of canoe falling *down* on us." He regarded the unconscious man solemnly. "Down from the surface of the third sea? Did *he* fall down from that future sea? Is that where he came from?"

"This fellow hasn't drowned," Harley growled.

"So maybe he held his nose under water," Highsmith retorted, and continued his study of the man in the sack. "Supposing he *did* live here after the glaciation, after this new ice is gone three or four or five thousand years from now; supposing he played in the mud and made bricks on the shore of Lake Agassiz, while his brother paddled around out there in his dugout canoe. Supposing something came between them? And maybe they weren't brothers or tribesmen, maybe they were enemies and the other fellow in the canoe caught this one and beat him up."

With sarcasm: "And burned him with that polygon?"

"That part doesn't fit, Harley—and neither does the knife. Brickmakers and canoeman can't have advanced weapons, unless they steal them from someone else."

"So fit a sophisticated enemy into your scheme."

"Well, yes, Harley—I'll do that for you; I'll have a brand-new theory for you in about five minutes. One sophisticated enemy coming up—one scientific slicker who knocks down mud-brick men with rubbery polygons and then tosses fine knives as consolation prizes."

The doctor was fussing over his mud-brick man but did not answer. Highsmith turned on the waiting woman.

"Maps, Jeanmarie. When we get back, will you order up some maps? I'd like old maps of the two nations, before Canada joined the Union. Maps showing the greatest extensions of the last two ice sheets—you said one of them reached almost to the Missouri River—and maps giving the boundaries of those two Agassiz seas. I want to see the ancient shorelines. I want to know just how much territory was covered by ice *and* water, and how much was spared; I want present-day locations of kames, moraines, and drumlins—everything pertinent to this situation. If Washington South can't supply them, get ordinary maps and we'll make our own. Can do?"

"The Geological Survey office has them on file."

"Good, ask for everything! I want a geographical picture of the last two glaciations, and then we'll put together a picture of the next one—*this* one."

"I stand in awe of genius," Harley said. "I do."

"You're sitting down."

"I'll stand, if you'll hold the patient's head."

"No, thank you. I think that head has fleas."

"Body lice," the doctor corrected.

"Well, whatever . . . " Highsmith watched the woman unconsciously brush her hands together and then wipe them on her parka. "Jeanmarie, that lake—those two lakes—were they really big?"

She nodded. "Agassiz was larger than all our Great Lakes combined; it may have been as large as Hudson Bay today. Many hundreds of rivers and streams in six states were dammed by the ice but the largest area of water covered Saskatchewan, Manitoba, and Ontario. An extension reached down as far as South Dakota, and into central Minnesota. Lake Winnipeg is all that remains today."

"And now it's frozen. What was the duration?"

"Each lake persisted for several thousand years. They were relatively quick to fill, but slow to drain as the climates warmed."

"Depth?"

"The depth is not known but they were thought to be shallow, as compared to any of the Great Lakes."

"And the old beaches—those ancient shorelines—are they out there now under the snow?"

"Yes, sir."

"You'd think the farmers and ranchers would have found them, seen them."

"They were found and mapped, but the configurations weren't recognized as beaches except by geologists and others in related disciplines. Soil deposits have transformed the whole area into farming and grazing districts, although sand hills and sand ridges persist throughout the area. In many places excavators have tapped the underground sand and gravel deposits for building materials, and in some few places the old shorelines are sufficiently close to the surface to be photographed from the air."

"Think of it, Jeanmarie: in another five or eight or ten thousand years all this will be sea again, and we can all go down to the beach on a Sunday afternoon for a picnic and a swim."

"If the new lake extends this far westward."

"Yes, that. Our base and Regina will be sitting on the bottom of the sea—on the bottom of Lake Agassiz the Third. That's a strange thought." His glance strayed to the man in the thermal sack, attracted by movement there. "And *that* poor devil had the bad luck to get into a fight on the beach; he lost and fell down on us. I wish we could have seen his opponent."

"The evidence suggests a different type of opponent."

"*Much* different—someone incredibly superior to him in almost every way. Why are they picking on him, on the other sixteen who came down earlier?"

"Historically, the superior people have always assaulted and conquered the inferior ones found in their way." She looked at Seventeen and back to Highsmith. "I mean superior in the sense of intelligence, training, arms, and means of transportation, not necessarily physical strength or native cunning."

"Understood. What's happening to him, Harley?"

"He's coming around, he is!"

Seventeen groaned in his sack and struggled to fight free of it, but only his remaining arm responded to his will. A balled fist punched at the encumbrance, seeking a way out, and sluggish moments later his feet kicked at the bottom of the bag in an effort to break through. The doctor hurriedly opened the thermal down to the man's waist and grasped the flailing hand, gently leading it free of the loose covering. Highsmith caught a glimpse of an incredibly dirty stomach and a tight band of something wrapped around the abdomen; he thought it might be a loin guard. Blood from the new wound flowed down his arm to mix with the dirt there.

That sinewy arm came out of the sack and stretched full length, stretched with new freedom as the fingers curled in an instinctive motion. Highsmith imagined they were curling over the hilt of the knife, or grasping a club. Movement stopped. The fingers were hooked on the sleeve of the doctor's garment.

Seventeen held himself rigidly still and it was easy to think of tactile impressions racing up the length of his arm. Then the fingers moved in examination while the shaggy head began a slow rolling motion. Highsmith hitched closer in anticipation, eager to see the awakening.

The doctor handed him the cardiogun and reached for his medical kit.

Jeanmarie said: "His eyes are open!"

Jeanmarie was brutally slammed the length of the cabin, crying at the unexpected hurt. A balled fist struck her with brutish force and knocked her backward along the aisle—struck so quickly and savagely that the words were just spoken as the blow fell. She tumbled at the pilot's feet and lay still. Seventeen grappled with the sack and tried to fight free, to follow her; he raised himself on his one good arm and began a lurching movement from a sitting position, then sought to brace himself up with the other arm that was no longer there. He fell back to the deck, struck the fresh stump, and howled with blinding agony.

"Pin him," Harley cried. "Pin him down!"

Highsmith came down quickly on the remaining arm and shoulder, frightened of the man but quick to obey the doctor. Seventeen struggled to throw him off. The doctor jabbed a hasty needle into the pinned arm and pushed. The three of them thrashed together on the deck.

The pilot trimmed his engines and dropped toward the lighted runway with reckless haste. Jeanmarie lay unconscious at his feet. He was more concerned for her than for anything happening behind him.

Highsmith shouted hoarsely over the bellowing man. "There's his enemy, Harley! *She* is the enemy!"

SIX
—
Iron

The trackers followed the twin swaths and the marching army into the valley and cautiously slowed their pace, moving warily now because they were plainsmen who felt ill at ease when hemmed in by the ridged hills to either side. Visibility and safety were restricted here. The quarry ahead of them always kept scouts out to protect their flanks and to maintain a watch before and behind. The valley could become a sudden trap.

The young trackers were brothers, separated by a year or two in age but so alike in physical appearance

they could have been born only minutes apart. They
shared a common skill but that skill was scarcely needed
now. The marching company was easy to follow because
of their great number and because of the rubbish they
left behind them; the company made no attempt at concealment and they hadn't bothered to bury their debris,
an incredible array of castoff food, ashes from their
fires, personal tokens, and excrement. The trackers considered them foolish.

They were doubly easy to follow because of the double swaths cut through the grass by the strange-shaped
thing which moved with a life of its own. That *thing* was
a frightening marvel. Grass was mashed flat under it and
behind it, forming two identical trails a certain distance
apart; the brothers could leap from one swath to the
other but they could not touch both at once when lying
on the ground between the tracks, arms outstretched.
They had first picked up the twin trails when the alien
object passed through a timber now many days behind,
and then had followed it out onto the plains with an
ever-increasing curiosity. The trackers could not guess
the kind of animal responsible.

First sight of the thing itself was numbing.

It was larger than any animal and it moved alone; no
one pulled it or pushed it and no one seemed to guide it,
unless the solitary individual sitting on top had something to do with the guidance. It rolled forward on four
round objects like circular stones positioned beneath it,
objects which turned without rest until the marching
troop paused to rest; it rolled without noise and without
droppings and it was so heavy the grass was pushed
down. An armed band of scented women marched before it and alongside it, always watching their scouts on
forward point. The brothers were equally astonished at
the prisoners. A band of captives walked immediately
behing the unfamiliar thing, captives bent under heavy
loads of firewood. They followed after the extraordinary
thing with little or no fear of it, and if a laggard fell behind he or she was quickly prodded by the armed guard
bringing up the rear of the long column.

The trackers discovered them all on the plains and fell in a safe distance behind, their eyes and imaginations turning now on the captives. Their stealthy pursuit was slowed only when the company entered a long valley and the trackers felt themselves surrounded by the confining hills. They were alert for traps.

A sharp cry and the shrilling of a whistle halted the company for a paralyzed moment, and then it exploded into action. The trackers dropped into the concealing grass a distance away from the swaths and waited with sudden alarm, fearing they were discovered. They were not. Ahead of them the scouts on point were examining something heaped on the shore of a small pond or lake, something not visible at this distance but something generating excitement. Two of their number turned and climbed the adjoining hill, running up a game trail with what speed they could muster. They shouted again when they reached the top and one of them uttered an angry cry which seemed to change to an anguished scream. Others climbed the hill.

Good visibility was hindered by rocks strung out along the top of the ridge, but to the watching brothers it appeared that some of the first to reach the top had dropped to their knees and placed their hands on the ground before them, as if in prayer to their gods. They rested in that position for a long moment while tortured screams continued somewhere beyond them, somewhere over the ridge, and then they were up again and running down the other side. The entire company had come to a halt in the valley, with the captives bunching up behind the rolling thing for protective safety.

The distant screaming was suddenly chopped off, and in the new silence the first of the troops came straggling back over the ridge carrying two inert burdens between them. Those burdens were brought down the game trail and deposited near the heaped mount beside the pond. A knot of onlookers gathered around the place. The two trackers rested in the grass and watched with wary readiness, keenly aware that the wind was carrying their scent down to the troop. They waited an interminable time while the sun inched across the afternoon sky.

After a while the company moved forward again in the same manner as before, as though nothing had happened. The lumbering, rolling thing went forward in its usual place and the body of prisoners tagged along after it, all of them pressing on to a huge lake or sea beyond the valley.

At nightfall the trackers left their hiding places and followed the twin swaths toward the distant water, knowing an increased security in darkness. There was no moon, but familiar stars were in the sky and those stars helped limn the ridges which threatened to close in on them. A clean wind was at their backs, offering additional security—no other enemy followed them into the valley. They ran along the swaths on bare and silent feet, alert for guards or sentries who might have been left behind. A short distance up the valley near the game trail they found a cold-water pond and paused to drink, then discovered a heaped mound of fresh mud now half dried under the sun. Nearby but well above the waterline they found two other mounds of freshly turned dirt, and a quick exploratory dig into one of them disclosed a woman's body buried there. There were no useful tools or weapons hidden in the grave and the brothers covered it again, taking care to leave no marks of their invasion.

They pressed forward.

The enveloping ridges dropped away abruptly and they were out on the plain once more, a new grassland that swept down to the shores of the inland sea. The company had camped there, again with no attempt at concealment; their fires ringed the shore and the people themselves were spread out to a great distance away from the water as they prepared to bed down for the night.

The trackers were startled by a flaring radiance.

A great and blinding light burned away the night, a painfully brilliant light brighter than the moon at *its* brightest; the light stabbed out from the middle of the camp to probe the outer darkness, moving along in a lazy half-circle about the encampment in search of something unseen. It seemed a living thing, a dangerous thing. The brothers burrowed into the concealing grasses and attempted to burrow into the soil beneath, half paralyzed by fright of the new wonder. The light crept toward them, searching for them, appearing to know they were there.

Two sentries were suddenly revealed in the glare, sentries who stood between them and the light source itself. They were so near the brothers would have run them down if they had not halted and dropped at sight of the radiance. The moving light found the sentries and stopped, holding there until one of them faced the source and made an easy signal of security. The second sentry began a turn as the light drifted away, retracing its early arc in the same lazy fashion. Both sentries watched it go. The blinding illumination washed the grasses along an invisible line until it reached the beach, where it played on the water for a time and blinked out. The brothers waited, but it did not come again.

On a silent signal from one of them, they rose to hands and knees and crept forward in stealthy silence.

A new barrier stopped them short.

It gave off a betraying odor, a strange smell never before experienced and that forewarned them before they crawled into it. The barrier appeared to be a novel kind of rope, a line not made of leather strips or braided grasses or any other kind of roping material they knew; it was solid and taut and was held off the ground on poles, a peculiar new type of guardian line reaching around the encampment as far as the eye could see by starlight. The sentries stood only a short distance away inside that barrier, silhouetted against the sky and the beach fires. An aromatic scent was strong on the night air. They had their backs turned, as they looked down on the fires and listened to the singing there.

They were dead before the end of the song.

Again on a silent signal the brothers rose up together and hurdled the barrier, throwing themselves at the unsuspecting sentries and leaping on their backs to seize the throats. The only sounds were a startled gasp, a quickly muffled cry, and then the two were falling with the brothers riding them to earth in brutal strangleholds they could not break. The struggle was brief. Two slim necks were snapped and the sentries went limp, as lifeless as that other woman found in the valley grave.

The brothers explored their bodies with excitement, stripping away the cloth coverings to see and feel the contoured flesh beneath. Tactile sensations were beyond power of description. The tantalizing scent was strong in their nostrils, goading their lust.

The two bodies were stripped of their possessions as the trackers made ready to leave, still intent on their original goal. The long knives were wonder weapons having incredibly sharp edges and points, and so well polished they appeared to reflect starlight; the black objects were puzzling because they had handles and holes and a smell that couldn't be identified, but they might be useful later; the pocket items and the talismans hanging about the necks were minor treasures to be wrapped in cloths taken off the bodies and carried away. Only the leathery pods encasing the feet were left, because they would not fit the brothers.

The trackers quit the scene and went in, searching for the captives who had followed the rolling thing.

A second barrier was found and surmounted, another line affixed to poles like that outer defense, but this one was more difficult to find because it was close to the ground at about the height of a man's foot. It was discovered in time only because the grass along it had been trampled its entire visible length where those who had strung it left sign of their own passage. The trackers stepped over the new line and pressed forward.

The goal was sighted.

The prisoners were revealed by their massed scent, a very different scent from that heady one worn by the women who carried the prized knives; this scent was a more common one, a long-familiar smell, and the trackers zeroed in on it to discover the captives bunched together in a quiet place far removed from their captors and the rolling marvel. They had been linked together with leather cords tied to their ankles to forestall escape and then set aside, well away from the center of camp. Some of them were eating while others were already stretched out in tired sleep, but a few—a very few—were sitting alert on their pallets looking out into the darkness where the brothers watched and waited. They had caught sight or smell of the incoming shadows.

The two shadows studied *them,* the few alert ones, and made their choices. They crept nearer.

One woman was selected, and then another. The new knives sliced out and cut the cords binding the ankles, as the captives watched in stunned disbelief. Some of those thought to be asleep stirred on their pallets and sat up to stare at the newcomers, at what the newcomers were doing. The stolen knives were easily recognized and fear mixed with astonishment swept the captive band. A shining knife was pointed at their throats, their mouths, and those mouths remained shut. The selections were made in silence. The selected women were pulled to their feet and guided through the huddled prisoners toward the outer darkness. The touch of a knife urged them along.

Night silence was rudely shattered.

A terrified scream tore the darkness at some far place, followed by a shrill, piercing whistle. A shouting was heard on the beach. The blinding light blazed up in the camp, seeming to come from the top of that strange rolling thing the brothers had tracked; a very bright beam of fire that stabbed across the encampment and picked out a group of people struggling at the water's edge. A crude boat was beached there and the figures limned by the light appeared to be fighting over the possession of it. Consternation reigned in the camp and then a number of shouting women converged on the scene, chasing a man who had clearly won the struggle and was now pushing out to sea in his captured boat. As before, some of those who pursued him had already dropped to their knees on the sandy shore and put their hands out before them in attitudes of supplication to their gods. The man in the boat hid himself.

The brothers were quick to take advantage of the diversion. They turned and ran into the enveloping night, ran toward the safety of the ridged hills they had first feared, carrying with them their stolen booty: two captive women, the wondrous knives, the trinkets and cloth taken from the bodies of the dead sentries, and finally the two small black objects which had the convenient handles on their tops. The brothers ran with confidence and elation, counting it a successful day.

The stolen women raced with them, frightened by the turn of events but pleased and gratified to be free, free of the captors who had taken them prisoner a long time ago when they were young. The women knew a heady, pounding exuberance they had not felt since before their capture.

They were among the hills.

One of the women fell after running blindly into a heaped mound of half-dried mud beside a pond. She failed to see it and cried out in alarm as she tumbled over it, coming to rest between two new graves. The man who had cut her bonds came back to help. He pulled her from between the graves and rebuked her by slapping her face, and then he piled his stolen treasures into her arms to hold while he stooped and quickly smoothed the soil over the graves to remove all traces of their passage. When he was satisfied he took back his new knife and turned to run again, striking the woman with the blade to urge her on. She ran with him, carrying his booty, but because she was afraid of being struck again she didn't let him know that she had dropped the sentry's gun.

SEVEN

Ice

A rising gale was blowing off the glacier.

Fisher Highsmith hugged the alien artifact to his breast and warily circled the aircraft, fighting the wind to stay on his feet. He had the unpleasant sensation of being watched, spied upon. The prickly sensation irritated the nape of his neck. He scanned the runway but it was deserted, and already the blowing snow was filling in the tracks of that noisy mob which had greeted their arrival. Highsmith turned to look behind him, searching the gusty spaces between the buildings, but no one watched him there. The frost-rimmed shop-windows were empty of faces, and even the wolf was gone from the fenceline.

It was likely the animal had been frightened out of its wits by the tumultuous arrival of the aircraft. They had touched down with a rattling thump and a screech in the undercarriage, the homecoming of an overanxious pilot.

Word had quickly gotten around. Almost every man on the base who happened to be awake had rushed out into the runway to greet the craft and gawk at the lively corpse. Seventeen was the newest wonder of the Western world, and the sergeant in the tower said that already some bureaucrats from Washington South were planning to fly in on an inspection tour. Almost every man on the base who happened to be awake was now crowded into the corridor outside that small room which served as their hospital, eagerly awaiting developments. Many of them had helped carry the lively prize into the sick bay, but only a few stouthearted ones had stayed when Harley peeled away the temporary plastic bandage and began working on the shoulder stump. The doctor would look up from his patient after a while, discover the intruders for the first time, and throw them all out. He liked to run a tight hospital.

Highsmith had carried Jeanmarie into the dormitory and put her to bed. Harley had instructed him to leave her there with an analgesic and an ice bag; he would look in as soon as he could get away.

Afterward, Fisher Highsmith went back outside to the aircraft to retrieve his alien artifact, the rubbery polygon thing.

A chill northwest wind drove down from the glacier, pushing before it an ominous cloud cover that had already obscured the brillant moon of an hour or so before.

Highsmith plodded through the drifting snow to the nose of the aircraft and nearly tripped over the electric cable concealed just below the surface. He did a clumsy dance to recover his balance and then backed up against the fuselage to reconnoiter. The itching neck persisted. The unlighted windows of the tower caught his eye, and a moment later he picked out the face of the communications sergeant. *There* was the spy: the nosy fellow was sitting up there in the warm dark watching him. Highsmith plodded half again around the aircraft to put it between himself and the tower. A man needed privacy.

He thrust the alien weapon out at arm's length, aimed it at the distant fence, and squeezed the handle.

"Fire!"

No fire.

He tried a new and different grip on the handle.

"I said *shoot*."

No shot.

Highsmith gripped the offending handle with both hands and squeezed again.

"Fire, now!"

There was no responding thunderbolt, no lethal beam of anything leaping from weapon to fence.

Highsmith pulled off his insulated mittens to feel the weapon, to finger it from one end to the other. It was cold. He turned it about to peer into the maw but found nothing; there wasn't so much as a hopeful spark or a glowing coal in the pit of the weapon. Reversing the obstinate artifact, he held it in his two bare hands and struggled to crush the handle, or trigger, or whatever it was. The distant fence remained inviolate, but a shadowy movement there suggested the wolf had returned. With a growing frustration, Highsmith turned about and slammed the maw against the fuselage.

"*Make* a hole!" He pressed the handle and counted to five, then pulled away to inspect the damage.

The pilot would have no cause for alarm.

"Ah, to hell with it."

His fingers were cold and the gale winds threatened to penetrate his clothing and freeze his bones. Highsmith recovered the broken bow and the knife from the seat within the craft and beat a retreat. Above him in the darkened tower a curious sergeant leaned on a sill and watched him to the door. Whipped snow blew down the runway, covering his footsteps as soon as he left them. A hard northwest wind slammed against the buildings.

Fisher Highsmith entered the dormitory and made his way down the narrow aisle to Jeanmarie's bed. She was awake, although others slept around her in the darkened room. Highsmith hunkered down beside her, between her bed and the adjoining one.

"Hello. Has Harley been here yet?"

"No." Jeanmarie moved her head cautiously on the pillow to see him. "It hurts. Very sore."

"And it *will* be for a couple of days." He looked at the bruise. "Ever been knocked out before?"

"No."

"I have. Used to get into fights all the time when I was a kid. Old Seventeen has a grudge for you."

She only stared at him, unwilling to talk.

Highsmith said: *"You're* his enemy—his future enemy, did you know that? *You* are the antagonist from tomorrow, knocking down brickmakers and canoe paddlers. I told Harley that, but he doesn't believe me—he's a stubborn old northlander. Harley has no imagination, no brilliant intuition; he lacks the superior reasoning powers of a trained scientist like me. I mean, like us. You and me." Highsmith sat down on the floor between the beds and again inspected the swollen jaw. He thought the discoloration added something to her fairness. "That's a beauty. You'll be on a mush diet for a while."

When she failed to reply, he hitched himself closer to her pillow and then used a corner of the bed sheet to wipe away a trickle of blood below her nostrils. "I had a nosebleed every time I got into a fight. I don't mean the other guy whipped me, I mean I always got excited and *that* started the nosebleed. It was a family curse."

Jeanmarie managed a weak nod.

Highsmith unbent his knees and stretched out his long legs under her bed, which brought him an inch or so nearer. He wondered what she'd do if he kissed her.

"Jeanmarie, if you feel up to it, you can sneak into sick bay after Harley leaves and punch the warrior in the nose. He's strapped in, and asleep."

She made a negative reply without words.

"Well, maybe not, but you *are* his enemy. That blue-eyed warrior found the three of us in the cabin when he came around but he ignored the two men who could have been his enemies, who *should* have been the enemy. He went for you. He assaulted the only woman on board, and that's significant, Jeanmarie. *You* are significant. I call that circumstantial evidence, a prime clue; I'll fit into the model I'm building.

"Never mind Mesopotamia—we'll ignore Mesopotamia and all that teleportation magic; the people living in Pan-Arabia today don't wear breechcloths and radiation burns. Harley said old Seventeen had a nasty burn on his back; they hit him from behind. They stabbed him and cut him and then burned him down when his back was turned. He's a temperate man, a temperate-climate man. He came from the last temperate climate, or the next one; it has to be the recovery period after the *last* ice age, or the period to come after *this* one."

Highsmith waited, but she offered no comment.

"It was a temperate zone, but a primitive period inhabited by primitive men. Tell me, does our blue-eyed warrior fit into the primitive period we know—into that period ten or twelve thousand years ago when the Asians crossed the Beringia land bridge to invade Alaska and Canada? Or even later, when the Amerinds inhabited this continent? *Is* he an Asian, or an Amerind?"

"No."

"I agree. He didn't live in *our* primitive past. And I think his enemy was a woman—women—armed with sophisticated weaponry, that polygon gun and the excellent knife. Do she or they fit into *our* primitive past?"

"No."

He gestured. "This ice. I'm building my model on this glaciation. He doesn't belong to the history we know, so he must belong to the history to come; to the new recovery period and the new warmth *after* this glaciation has ended. Somewhere up there, three or four or five thousand years from now primitive men are starting all over again, and civilized women are burning them down and bouncing them back on us." He studied the civilized woman on the bed. "But I'm willing to listen to any other theory. Do you have one?"

"No."

"Then we're stuck with mine." He used the corner of the sheet to wipe away another fleck of blood from her lip. "Am I boring you, Jeanmarie?"

"No."

"Good! I like your ideas. We may be sitting on the bottom of the next Lake Agassiz, we may be picking up the bodies and the pieces of future men and ravelins and dugout canoes falling down on us from that battle to come—Harley's lost battle. The casualties and the debris from a battle three or four or five thousand years away, maybe more, tumbling down on us after the glacier has retreated and primitive men have taken over this corner of the world again." His inquisitive gaze locked on hers. "I wonder if those civilized people are coming over to the new world from Europe *again*?"

No reply.

"Jeanmarie, why are you the enemy? What do you have against Seventeen? We know what he has against you, but why do you hate him?"

She moved her head on the pillow.

"That's what I thought," Fisher Highsmith said. "I wish I had the nerve to send all this down to Washington South."

She questioned him with her eyes.

"No," he replied. "I haven't sent down anything but the recovery data, and I asked for all those maps while I was at it."

"Did they acknowledge?"

"They did, they said the maps would be here by morning on the facsimile line. I'm not going to send down my theory—not just yet. They'd drum me out of the corps, and you'd have to break in a new man next week. The wisest course is to wait for the maps and use them—fit them into the theory and *then* send everything down." He snapped his fingers in sudden recall. "Oh, hey! We have visitors coming! The sergeant said some Washington people are flying up to see our catch."

"Be prepared for them."

"Will do. I'll practice saying, 'We're working on the problem, *sir*.' That ought to satisfy them a while longer." Highsmith picked up the artifact from his lap and held it above the level of the bed for her to see. "This damned thing won't work for me at all, not at all. I tried everything outside, but nothing happened." He pointed it at the ceiling and gripped the handle tightly. "See: nothing. Do you suppose old Seventeen will give me a hint?"

"Doubtful."

"No, I guess not—he shouldn't know how it works, he was only the poor primitive on the receiving end."

Highsmith slammed the polygon onto the floor on its butt end. "I damned near squashed this handle—"

The glimmering flash astonished him.

He had the sudden illusion of a climbing purple flash —no, not a flash, it wasn't really a flash, but a thin tenuous *blur* of something purple flung skyward in the blink of an eye. He did blink in stunned reaction and saw again the purplish blur on his eyelids. Something wraithlike hurtled skyward, and a fine powdery plaster came down on Jeanmarie's bed, followed by something else wet. He thought he was seeing melted snowflakes.

Jeanmarie cried, "Fisher!" and pointed up.

Highsmith gaped at the dormitory ceiling and saw a rounded hole there slightly larger than a balled fist. The hole was neatly cut and quite new; it hadn't been there a moment ago but now a mixture of snow and melting snow water trickled in. He snatched his hand back from the rubbery handle of the artifact and scrambled to his feet. A puddle was beginning to form on the floor, threatening to wet him. Displaying great presence of mind, Highsmith pushed the woman's bed away from beneath the hole and then turned to stare up at it anew. Snow from the outer storm drifted in.

"I think I'd better go and find a bucket."

Behind him in the doorway the doctor made a demand. "What did you do? Just what did you *do* here?"

"I fired this funny gun, that's what I did." He blew Jeanmarie a hasty kiss and ran along the aisle to the door. The doctor was shouldered aside without apology. "Harley—see if you can find a man to go up on the roof, send somebody up there to patch that hole—the glacier is coming down."

"Wait, wait," the doctor cried as Highsmith pushed past him.

"Jeanmarie will tell you!" And he was gone.

Harley stared at the woman and at the ruptured ceiling with amazement. "What is that fool doing now? What is he?"

"Proving his theory," she mumbled in response.

Highsmith stumbled through the deepening snow around the nose of the aircraft, but this time he remembered the electric cable and stepped carefully over it. He had been running as he left the building, running as he met the wintry blast in the open door, but the depth of snow quickly slowed his steps as the gale nearly flattened him. Highsmith eased along the fuselage to the tail section and huddled under the starboard elevator to conceal himself and his prize from the man in the tower. Very cautiously, he repeated the act performed a short while before: he held out the artifact at arm's length, aimed the muzzle at the distant fence, and squeezed hard on the trigger.

There was no response, no purplish blue.

Fisher Highsmith felt he had been robbed.

He spun around and banged the butt of the weapon against the fuselage, thumping it as smartly as he'd done in the dormitory, but again was disappointed. The polygon seemed to have gone on strike. He banged it against the craft a second time and squeezed with all his strength, but the only reponse was an explosion of breath. Fisher Highsmith held the weapon in his two hands and simply looked at it. The one burning image in his mind was that of a neat round hole in the ceiling above the bed.

It occurred to him then there *was* a difference, one small difference between that accident and this test.

Heedless of the inquisitive sergeant in the tower, Highsmith dropped on his knees and scraped away the snow until he had uncovered a reasonably clean and satisfactory patch of cold concrete. The wind threatened to cover it almost at once, but he hoarded the cleared space and made haste to put the butt on the weapon in the center of the patch. He stretched out full length on the snow, being careful to keep out of the line of fire, and gripped the handle. There was no hiss, zap, or clap, but the discharge startled him all the same. Despite his being prepared for something, despite his expectations, the climbing purple blur startled him—it was a half-seen streak of blurred lightning jumping skyward, a flash again repeated on his closed eyelids when he blinked in reaction. He jumped and his grip loosened on the handle.

Highsmith rolled over on his back to follow the streak upward, thinking perhaps he might see it collide with the

storm clouds. He was much too late for that. Looking
up at the tail assembly above his head, he found a new
hole. A section of the elevator and its attached stabilizer
was climbing slowly away from him, falling *upward*: a
neat rounded section of the tail assembly now lazily rising toward the sky. The two pieces climbed in slow motion, climbed in that same peculiar and drifting fashion
in which debris came down on the snowfields. The tail
piece appeared to have all the time in the world to reach
the clouds—gravity was nothing.

Highsmith gaped at them in open astonishment and
waited for the inevitable fall; he didn't believe it was
possible for *this* debris to sail all the way up to the cloud
cover. The pieces were floating away too slowly and
gravity would have to seize them at some near point.

Behind and above him the window of the tower was
slid open. "Look at those crazy things!" The sergeant
was hanging halfway out the window, his neck twisted
the better to see the sky overhead. "Look!"

"I *am* looking," Highsmith called back. "How am I
going to explain *this* to the pilot?"

"They've got to be riding an updraft!"

"We don't have an updraft here. Do you think the pilot will be sore?"

"How did that happen, Fisherman?"

The Fisherman stared after the receding tail pieces.
"We scientists are always experimenting. I'm worried
about the pilot."

"Damn!" the sergeant shouted. He was in danger of
falling out the window. "No, look at *that*!"

The neatly severed pieces of elevator and tail stabilizer faded from view. There was no turning point as gravity finally seized them, no hesitation and then a reversal
for a fast return to the snow-packed earth. The two
pieces simply sailed out of sight *before* they reached
the cloud cover, fading from visibility as nicely as the
second image of a double exposure fades off a moving
film.

Highsmith searched the sky until his eyes ached from
the stinging wind but the pieces did not come back to

him. He rolled over on his belly once more and stared at the alien artifact on the concrete.

"What have you got down there?" the sergeant yelled.

"A gun of some kind."

"Well, that's a hell of a gun, mister!"

Highsmith was inclined to agree with him.

After a while he realized he was terribly cold, and then he realized he was still stretched out full length on the snow below the aircraft. He must have been there for several minutes without knowing it, without being aware of his position. He took up the weapon and ran for the door.

There was no thought of sleep.

Fisher Highsmith was too excited at his discovery to sleep, but before going back to the shop to commence work he stopped off in sick bay to look in on Harley and his patient and then in the dorm to see Jeanmarie. The station was quiet and most of the rooms dark.

Seventeen was asleep or unconscious.

The warrior-brickmaker was strapped face down on his bed, but Highsmith didn't believe those straps were mere precautions to save him from tumbling out in his sleep. His shoulder stump was newly bandaged, and now there was a light rubbery covering over most of his back where the doctor had treated the burn. The brickmaker's body had been throughly cleansed of grime and the breechcloth had been removed and thrown away. Highsmith thought that a good thing—the breechcloth hadn't been the most sanitary garment in the world.

Across the small room in the only other bed Harley was sleeping fully clothed on top of the blankets. The doctor revealed his weariness even in sleep. A pungent hospital smell filled the room, an odor of something vaguely unpleasant that seemed to cling to the roof of the mouth. Highsmith closed his mouth and backed out. The corridors were deserted.

Lights were out in the dormitory and most of the beds were occupied. With that brief excitement in sick bay ended, all of the station personnel not on night duty had gone to bed. Highsmith raised his glance to inspect the ceiling. Someone had covered the hole in the roof to keep out the storm but the ceiling repair job had been put off until morning. He found Jeanmarie's bed in the gloom by wandering along the aisle until he was beneath the hole. Highsmith squeezed in between her bed and the next one and then sat down on the cold floor in the same position as before, his long legs extended under the bed.

She was awake and holding an ice bag to her jaw.

Highsmith leaned forward until his face was almost touching hers on the pillow. "Feel better?"

"No." The reply was muffled by the ice bag.

"That's the spirit. I've been making progress, I've added another factor to the model I'm building."

He waited for a reply but there was none.

"I've discovered how the weapon works—well, not really how, but *when* it works, and I've experimented with some . . . ah, debris. I've duplicated the phenomena from the snowfields, you might say. The thing has to be grounded, Jeanmarie. Grounded here on the floor, which is concrete on a gravel base, I suppose, or grounded out there on the runway. The natural way would be to place it on the ground, aim at the enemy, and *wham*, he's done."

"Seventeen?"

"Seventeen got it in the back in one of two ways. He was huddled down behind his ravelin when they found him and blasted him and the ravelin off the earth—his earth—or they caught him running away and fired at his back. Don't ask how he got here with the polygon and a knife in his hand. I haven't worked that out yet. Do you have any ideas?"

"No."

"When that gun is fired the object before it is not only burned, it is blown out of existence. I don't mean blown into little bits and pieces, disintegrated, but literally blown out of the here and now into some other there and then. I've just experimented with that. I saw it happen. Maybe you saw it happen." He indicated the ceiling. "Jeanmarie, have you ever heard of a time gun? Is there any mention in the libraries?"

"No."

"I haven't heard either, but that seems to be what we have here. Seventeen was hit by a blast from his enemy's polygon gun and hurled *back* here on us; it knocked him out of a canoe or off a rock—wherever he was at, at the time—and dumped him back here on us because we were below him and behind him when he tumbled. Follow that? We were several meters below him in space and several thousand years behind him in time when he was gunned down. I mean *his* space, his primitive world up there after this ice age. He could have been standing on a moraine or a drumlin or paddling around on the lake surface—things that will be above where we are now after the glaciation. All the debris just floats and falls *down* on us."

The woman said nothing.

"If we're located on the bottom of Lake Agassiz the debris is sinking down through the water to us, but if we are in a valley between drumlins or moraines the pieces —and the men—are falling down the hillsides." He spread his hands on the bed sheet, smoothing it. "All depends on where we are now, with respect to the topography three or four or five thousand years in the future. We may be just below some future hanging valley —below the mouth of it—or we may be positioned at the foot of a terminal moraine; we may be in the valley between a pair of drumlins or we may actually be underground—damned if I know, Jeanmarie.

"I don't know what this country will look like a few thousand years from now when the glacier retreats, but we can't be located on *top* of anything—moraine, drumlin, arete, or esker—because everything is coming *down* on us. Down from a height and down from the future, after the glacier has created a whole new topography." And he paused to ask again: "Any ideas?"

"Not now."

"Every previous glaciation *has* created a new topography, *has* created new moraines and drumlins?"

"Yes."

Highsmith nodded his satisfaction. "The next one will be no different; I have to keep building on that. I think Harley was right: these men *are* coming in like stragglers from a lost battle, but they aren't really stragglers —they're casualties. Sixteen dead men plus one more near death. Primitive people who steal better weapons and get killed for their trouble. In their own lifetimes they ranged the high country that will be here after the ice is gone, they built ravelins on hillsides and fought and died over them—or behind them—because their enemies had the advantage.

"They could be survivors living on the edge of the ice sheet, hill men of the first thousand years after the ice, making a foolish stand against the invaders pushing in from outside. Civilization, if we may call it that, carrying polygon fire up from the south to reclaim these northern states. You said that civilized invaders have always used the traditional methods to steal land from the natives, so it's reasonable to believe our descendants will reclaim *this* land the same way our ancestors did. We're getting the casualties from that battle to come and I can't say I like it."

She murmured: "Losers."

Highsmith agreed. "The primitive men are losing because they are relying on mud-brick ravelins, Yakut bows, and maybe even slingshots for all I know. Our teams haven't picked up any slings yet, but give them a little time. It's a poor way to defend your land against *this*." He held up the rubbery artifact and then glanced at the ceiling. "You can't buck firepower that burns you, kills you, and pushes you out of existence—out of your year into somebody else's year. I'll say one thing for this gun: it makes for a neat and clean battlefield. Nothing to clean up afterward and no burial squads needed."

Jeanmarie said hurtfully: "He had weapons."

"We can be sure of the knife, Search Three said he had the knife in his hand when he fell down. The gun came down with him, immediately after him, but we don't know—" Highsmith hesitated to consider the possibilities. "All right, let's concede that; until we find evidence to the contrary let's concede he also had the gun in hand, but dropped it when he fell. There are bits and pieces of *another* weapon out in the shop that I couldn't begin to fit together because I couldn't guess the shape. That's the damnedest shape! Let's say that at least two of the defenders have been caught with guns in hand and *then* blasted out of existence. Let's build on that."

"Raids."

"Raids on the enemy, yes. Seventeen looks mulish enough to go up against a bull moose."

"Camp stores," Jeanmarie said. "Arsenals."

"Raids on an enemy camp could account for their possession of weapons, or the ambushing of a small force out in the open country, or even hand-to-hand combat with an individual—before reinforcements arrived to gun down the victor as he was running away. Any number of likely situations. Seventeen could have got *his* that way; he could have jumped somebody found on *his* hill and fought her to a standstill. Remember the beating he took while he was doing it, remember the cuts and stabs. He would have grabbed up the loser's knife and gun and run for his life—until somebody else, another of the enemy, popped over the hill behind him and shot him down." Highsmith looked down at the weapon. "I wonder if the poor devil learned how to use it before he was hit."

"No present evidence."

"No—there isn't. We've never picked up a fair-haired invader from the southland, or a wagon or mcahine or whatever kind of vehicle they travel in." He pretended to inspect the ice bag and then looked up into her eyes. "The search teams have never picked up a female."

She said only: "I don't question your theory."

"That's because you're a good polylib—but on the other hand you haven't supported it with enthusiasm."

"Not my responsibility to do so."

"True," Highsmith said. "But I'm building on that until a better idea comes along, until something utterly new turns up out there on the snowfields." He touched her fingers on the sheet. "*You* have the sore jaw—not me, not Harley, not the pilot. And Harley was touching him, holding his hand, but nothing happened to Harley. Nothing happened to me. You got the punch. He recognized *you* as the enemy, Jeanmarie."

She made no reply.

Highsmith gently stroked her fingers. "I can't say you're the Amazon type, but you don't need to be when you're toting that gun. All you need to do is ground it and fire it, drop to your knees or your stomach and squeeze the handle. The opponent is pushed right out of sight, pushed off the hill and out of the daylight he lives in, or on, on top of, or whatever. You win."

After a while Highsmith lifted his head to study the hole in the ceiling. He had to admit it was a neat cut.

"What do you suppose your old historian thought of *that*? Old what's-his-name, Fort? I wonder what he thought when a heap of plaster from our ceiling and a few tiles from our roof fell down out of the sky in his century?" The vivid image of a section of tail assembly came to mind, the image of that section slowly falling up and away out of the present time. The image also reminded him that he must notify the pilot and the shop mechanics.

"What do you suppose that old historian thought when some of my debris fell on him three or four hundred years ago? What did those primitive Canadian Indians think when it rained down on them four or five thousand years ago?" Fisher Highsmith contemplated her fingers, now resting in his hand. He couldn't remember ever touching Jeanmarie before, except to shake hands when they met, and to help her in and out of the aircraft. He wondered quickly if she had a lover on the station. "There's no guessing when the trash fell, not where but when. Three hundred years ago? Three thousand? I don't know; I can't guess. I'd have to know the duration of *this* ice to track our debris backward a comparable length of time—and that would be pretty rough tracking at best."

Jeanmarie took the ice bag from her face and spoke slowly through hurting lips.

"I will study his book carefully. There has not been time to read it all, and I don't know if the second half has been transmitted. Please ask the sergeant."

"I'll ask him. Jeanmarie, I'd be very pleased if you *did* find it recorded; I'd be delighted to have those roof tiles turn up in 1825, or somewhere! We'd know that *we* made history."

"The time span will not fit your model."

Highsmith considered that and had to agree. "The time span would knock the underpinnings from my model. I need several thousand years to build anything worthwhile, so I guess those old Canadian Indians will have to find the tiles. I don't suppose *that* will be in the book."

"Not likely."

"We just lost our chance in history."

"Yes, sir."

Fisher Highsmith released her hand with reluctance. She shouldn't have used the word "sir"; it neatly destroyed the romantic mood that had been building up within him. He pulled the sheet and blankets up under her chin and got to his knees.

"I'm going out to the shop to work on the ravelin; I want to put a complete ravelin together and then take old Seventeen out there to see it. I want to see *him* when he sees *it*. That ought to be good."

"The doctor may not permit that."

"Then I'll build a ravelin right there in sick bay. Harley can't stop scientific reconstruction, he can't stop progress. And then I'll put together *another* weapon from the pieces in the shop—I'll fake it, give it the proper weight and feel, and let Seventeen find it behind the ravelin. I'll arrange a confrontation! I *have* to see that man's reaction to know if I'm right about all of this."

"Yes, sir."

"Jeanmarie, I need your cooperation."

"How?"

He studied her for a long moment. "I want you there

for the confrontation, Jeanmarie. I want you there when it happens—when anything happens. If our primitive old warrior drops down behind that ravelin and fires that gun at you—not at me, not at Harley—but fires at *you*, well, I'll put all my evidence and maps together and send it down to Washington South. Problem solved."

The woman didn't appear terribly pleased.

"The gun will be a fake, Jeanmarie. Just pieces I'll put together with something inside to lend weight."

She made no reply.

"You won't be hurt again, Jeanmarie. Harley and I will be there to protect you."

She replaced the ice bag on her face.

From behind, a hard collection of knuckles rapped Highsmith on the shoulder. He turned on his knees to look at a bearded face raised an inch above its pillow.

"I'm trying to sleep, blabbermouth," the owner of the bearded face told him. "I worked hard all day, I've got more work piled up ahead of me tomorrow. Can you take a hint, gabby?"

"I can take a hint," Highsmith assured him.

"Then take it *now*, dammit!"

Fisher Highsmith wandered into the deserted shops and turned on the lights. His workbenches were along one wall, separated from the space given over to the mechanics and the maintenance crew. Sleds and spare gear for the search parties were stowed at the far end near large double doors providing egress to the frigid world outside. A few subdued rectangles of light spilled through the frosty windows, illuminating the snowy runway and a part of the standing aircraft. Highsmith made gloomy note of the fact that the tail section was clearly visible. A driving northwest wind constantly buffeted the craft and the block buildings behind it. He turned to his benches.

The reconstructionist had fitted only two bricks together when the pictophone summoned him. The curious face of the sergeant was there.

"I saw the lights, Fisherman. Thought you had gone to bed."

"Not yet, Sergeant, not yet. Hard at work here."

"Got time for the latest word?"

"What is it, good news?"

"Not all that good. Search One called in again about fifteen or twenty minutes ago and they're having a hard time. Debris is still coming down in Regina."

"A hard time from what?"

"The storm—this blizzard. And wolves."

"Didn't you say they were moving downtown?"

"I said that. They're somewhere near the center of town and still coming this way, but it's slow going. The blizzard is holding them down and now they've got a wolf pack trailing them."

Highsmith worried about his canoe fragment. "When were they due in here?"

"About sunrise—but they won't make it now."

"Can we help them?"

"If they need help I'll send Search Two."

"Two? Where is Search Two?"

The sergeant said: "Downstairs asleep." He gave the impression of wanting to add something else, something concerning Highsmith's intelligence.

Highsmith said: "Oh." He'd forgotten the fact. "What is Search One finding now?"

"Stones and fish."

The reconstructionist dropped his bricks. "Stones and fish? *Fish?*"

"That's what I said. Kind of funny, isn't it? Small stones, gravel, and dead fish."

Highsmith stared at the communications sergeant. "Charles Fort would appreciate that."

"I don't know Fort. Is he an enlisted man?"

Highsmith neglected to answer. His imagination was already painting a lurid picture of himself—and of the fully inhabited base—squatting on the muddy bottom of Lake Agassiz amid the debris floating down from the far future: pieces of canoe, gravel, dead fish, perhaps a frog or two, all settling to the bottom of the great inland sea which would exist here some thousands of years from now. He could almost look up through the waters to the surface of that sea and watch the struggle taking place there.

"Eighteen should be next, Sergeant—we should expect the man in the canoe next. The poor devil must be taking a beating."

EIGHT

Iron

The hunter and his woman trailed a lynx along the winding ridge of an esker, always working into the wind. The smell of the cat was strong ahead of them.

The hunter had first caught sight of the animal at daybreak when it broke cover, deserting the timber growing on the sunward side of the esker and climbing to the top of the grassy ridge. The cat had rested in the morning sun for a long time, disdainful of cover, while it listened to the wind and watched the plains below for sound or sight of a meal. The hunter and his woman squatted in the underbrush at the treeline, not daring to break their own cover until the cat moved; they were so close to the animal they could already smell it on the gentle south wind blowing to them. The esker twisted and turned like a wayward river, winding across the wide plains toward a range of hills in the far distance. The hunters and the hunted were separated by only one twist of the ridge.

The lynx moved when the sun was a space above the horizon and at once the hunter and his woman were after it. They left their hiding place in the underbrush and raced across an open field to the next bend of the esker, wisely following the cat's own path up the hill to keep themselves downwind of the animal. The grassy bed where it had rested for so long was still warm to their feet, and there was new urine in the bed. The lynx was not in sight. The hunter motioned the woman to a place behind him so that she would not obstruct the scent, and set out on the trail at an easy trot. They tracked the beast without a betraying sound, keeping to the thinning grass on the backbone of the ridge and sometimes circling the scrawny underbrush to avoid breaking twigs or sweeping against the leafy branches. The esker twisted a crooked course, now running into the sun and now away from it, but always following the southerly direction the melt-water river had followed when this land was beneath a stagnating ice sheet.

The hunter caught brief glimpses of his prey when the ridge would double back almost upon itself, and when the trees on the sunward slopes were so stunted as to allow a clear sighting from one ridgetop across to the other. He would fall to his belly in the grass and his woman would tumble at his feet. Together they would watch the cat on the adjoining ridge until it was gone from sight, and then they would be up and running to gain ground on it.

A sign of man stopped them in midstride.

They came upon the wall without warning just after rounding another turn, just after spotting the cat another time and realizing they were closing in on it. The animal was still unaware of them and in their hasty pursuit they almost overran the man-made barrier before discovering it.

The wall was built of mud bricks and was positioned just off the top of the ridge, a few paces down the sunny side of the slope; it commanded a good view of the plain below as well as a treeless section of the slope itself. The hunter knew that wall, knew the kind of man who made it, and knew what it was used for. He threw himself down in an instinctive motion and crawled forward on hands and knees, but he had already been reassured that no enemy waited for *him* behind the wall. The cat had gone by the trap without trouble, and there was no telltale odor of man before him. It was an old wall, one that had weathered many rains; there were signs of age in the sagging ends of the walls and in a few crumbling bricks that had fallen from place. His nose again confirmed the long abandonment: there was no remaining smell of man on the backside of the wall, where once a man had huddled and waited for game to come to him.

The hunter sprang to his feet and tested the wind, searching for the cat or any other living thing on the ridge. With a wary caution he searched the winding esker behind him, knowing that his own scent was being carried downwind. When he was satisfied, when his straining senses told him he was alone but for the woman and the cat, he turned back to the trail and hurried to make up for lost time. The woman rose up from her crouching posture and ran after him, carrying his bow and the few arrows they possessed.

They overtook the cat about midmorning, when it stopped again to sun itself and to resume the search for a meal on the plain below. The sudden strong odor of its nearness warned them and the hunter quickly left the ridgetop, to drop downslope into the concealing timber before going on. The lynx was discovered atop a great stone, a glacial boulder lying half buried in the sandy soil of the esker. The animal had to be taken there.

The hunter's woman was set out as bait.

She gave the bow and the basket of arrows to the hunter and crept forward through the timber, moving as stealthily as the underbrush would permit. She knew the role she was to play and experience had taught her to play it well. When she was a distance away from the man and at a place where the cat could catch scent of her, where it would have to turn and look at her, she walked out of the trees and began a slow and labored climb up the hillside. The woman gave no sign she knew the cat was on the rock.

The lynx spun around and flattened on its stomach, watching the woman and measuring the danger she posed. The long body squirmed in a betrayal of nervousness.

The hunter fitted an arrow to his string and crept up the slope to block a retreat, the ridgetop being best for a fight. He was behind the animal now and he watched it closely for a sign. The nervous squirming was only a first reaction. This animal stalked small game and birds; it liked to crouch on the lower limbs and drop down out of a tree onto the smaller animals below, or pounce on timid deer at waterholes, and sometimes it would climb high into the trees to rob nests or pick off sleeping birds —but the hunter couldn't guess what it would do *now*. The bait was larger than its usual victim. If the cat was driven by hard hunger it would jump the woman as she neared the rock, but if it was not desperate—if it had eaten during the night—it would turn tail when the bait came too close for comfort. The woman's path up the hill was calculated to force a decision. She carried only a bone knife concealed in her hand.

The hunter lifted his bow and took aim.

The cat lost its nerve and turned to run. In the space of a breath it discovered the hunter, spit at him, and whirled again to jump the woman. She was below it now and she thrust out the slender bone knife at the animal, screaming her defiance of it. The hunter fired, and missed. The arrow struck the rock below the cat and broke.

The lynx spun again, making only a quarter-circle, and launched itself from the boulder into the undefended space between the man and woman now closing in on either side of the rock. The hunter hurled his spear at the airborne target and caught the cat in midleap, caught it between two ribs, and the animal screamed its agony. It struck the ground rolling and running, snapping the shaft in two, and then gained its footing to hurtle down the slope toward the safety of the trees. The remaining half of the spear clung between the animal's ribs. The hunter and his woman plunged down after it, jubilant now that the battle was half won. Their cries added to the cacophony.

A uniformed woman rested on one knee just inside the shaded trees, watching the drama race toward her. One hand gripped the handle of a weapon and she kept a bead on the man running down the slope, but she was careful not to let the weapon touch the ground just yet. She held her fire and waited, wanting to see the outcome.

The cat was getting away, despite his handicap.

The hunter shouted at his woman and gestured wildly, ordering her away at an oblique angle into the timber. He changed his own course, wanting to be ahead of the animal. The bleeding cat would not run straight through the trees and out onto open plain beyond; it would turn and run one way or the other, upwind or downwind, but always within the confines of the timber for concealment. With the hunter's woman upwind, an obvious threat, the cat would turn another way and run downwind into the waiting hunter—onto the knife of the waiting hunter, who knew now he would have to fight the animal to take him. His bow and his few remaining arrows were behind him on the ridge, his only spear was broken, with half of it dangling in the cat's hide. He thought he could use *that* to advantage.

The wounded lynx reached the timber and vanished.

The hunter reached it only a moment later and ran a few short paces into the waiting shade, and stopped short. His head was up but the odor of cat and blood eluded him. Something interferred—some puzzling new scent. It was a heady scent, a tantalizing *new* scent that seemed so close it blotted out every other smell that should be present. He turned into the wind seeking a source.

A woman was kneeling on the ground before him only a short distance away, staring at him, measuring him, and he mistook her position for one of submission. *She* had the new scent. He marveled at that and at the strange garments covering her body, but at the same time he wondered why she would want to cover herself in such fashion. He peered half around the woman and found her feet encased in some other kind of covering. The day was not that cold.

A sound and a movement behind the stranger caught his eye, and the cat was upon them. The hurtling animal was half blinded by pain and a berserk fury.

It struck the kneeling woman and bowled her over because she was unprepared, because she neither sensed nor heard the oncoming beast. The hunter marked that against her. He thrust out his knife and jabbed the empty air in a bellyslashing motion, taunting the cat. It screamed at him and mauled the flattened woman as the claws dug in for a leap. The hunter shouted and stepped forward in a feint. The cat launched itself at the standing enemy and they came together with an explosive sound, a blow that knocked the hunter backward. He tumbled over, taking the cat with him and letting it fall upon the upthrust blade. The animal clawed viciously at his arms and thighs, struggling to break free, but the hunter dug his knife into the feline body and savagely held it there while his free hand groped over the body seeking the broken shaft of spear. He raised his legs and attempted to lock them around the struggling animal but failed a purchase. They rolled on the ground and the claws of one foot caught the back of his neck and tore open a shocking wound down his spine. One of them screamed.

The hunter found the broken shaft when the cat got all four feet onto the ground and began to run. The man was dragged with it for a very short distance until the animal dropped in death, its stomach and lung ripped apart. The hunter rolled away and managed to raise himself up on his hands in time to see the final sign. The cat was dead but the body continued twitching until the muscles went limp.

The woodlands were hushed.

After a long while the hunter climbed to his knees and looked around for his women. The movement shot a searing pain down his back and backbone but he clamped his teeth together to hold back the cry and searched for the women. He found the first one—the familiar one—half concealed behind a stump some distance away; she was crouched there and staring at the newcomer with a mixture of fear and ill-humor. The hunter knew that look. He turned his head to stare at the woman with the penetrating scent and found *her* on hands and knees crawling slowly toward him. That woman was bleeding from her wounds and the smell of running blood was mixed with the intoxicating scent of her body. The new woman was searching for something lost in the weeds and stringy vines of the woodland floor. The fine cloth hung from her body in tatters.

The hunter tried to get to his feet and discovered that he could not. He fell back to a sitting position and bellowed to his woman, the familiar woman, to come to him. She crept halfway around the stump and hesitated.

The newcomer found what she was searching for and picked up a little black object from its nest in the vines. She held it out toward the hunter, offering it to him, and carefully placed it on the ground in front of her. Both her hands were gripping it.

He thought he heard his own woman cry out.

The two women reached the shoreline of the great sea just after sunset, at the end of a daylong march.

The older one, the hunter's woman, was a captive and she had learned that servitude at the point of a knife pricking her backbone during the trek. It was hardly a march. The journey should have taken only half as long. They had quit the treeline at the base of the esker while the sun was still on the slope, not yet overhead, and had walked across the plain at a slow and faltering pace because the new woman could not keep up. She was weak. She had difficulty in remaining upright and difficulty in walking; she was a contemptuous object to the prisoner because she had not fought back against the cat, and she lacked the strength now to carry meat or walk proudly away from the kill. They were degrading signs. The prisoner bided her time and waited for an opening, waited for the moment when the knife that reflected sunlight or the small black weapon were not at her back.

They had crossed the plain under the bright sun and then turned toward the great water when they came up against the hills. The new woman could not climb the hills and so they turned to go around them, making the journey even longer. The shining knife was always there, always urging the hunter's woman forward.

She felt trickles of blood on her backside.

The sun had set but it was not yet dark when they reached the sea. The captive dropped down at the edge to drink from cupped hands and to scrub her face in the icy water. When she was done she turned to look at the tiny fires burning along the shoreline a great distance away, and guessed that was their destination: a tribe of weaklings like this one.

This one was kneeling at the water's edge washing the dried blood from her body where the cat had left its mark. She had taken off the tattered cloth from the upper part of her body and that body was sickly white when the blood and grime were gone. The hunter's woman found it hard to believe that whiteness.

The other woman called to the captive and motioned her to come closer. She held the knife and the black thing in one hand and tried to rinse away the blood from her back with the other, but the free hand could not cup water and carry it back without spilling. She wanted her back washed. The captive knelt at her back with a double handful of icy water and scrubbed at the wounds. The younger woman cried out at the sudden pain of it, and threatened with the knife. The hunter's woman jumped back.

They waited a moment, captor and captive, and then came a second order to rinse the clawed flesh. The captive slowly and carefully filled her two hands with water and patted the white skin free of muck, letting the cold water trickle through her fingers in soothing fashion. She was gentle about it, feigning a tenderness. The younger woman made a small murmuring sound and sighed, causing the captive to bend around her and look into her face. A silent question. The quick nod, and another but less imperative gesture was the answer. The captive gathered up fresh water.

Holding the water in her two cupped hands, she stood up quickly without a betraying sound and kicked the newcomer into the icy sea. It was a hard blow to the base of the skull, intended to kill, and the victim tumbled forward with a screeching gasp. Her knife and the black thing fell to the ground. The captive, now the attacker, scrambled for the weapons.

A brilliant flash and the sudden roiling of water startled the hunter's woman, frightened her so thoroughly that she loosed the black thing and jumped away, running back a dozen strides from the sea's edge. The newcomer, the weakling, had vanished. There seemed to be a churning hole in the water itself and the new woman had fallen into that roiling hole and disappeared, as surely as her own mate had disappeared many hours before. The water continued to swirl, creating a storm within itself.

The hunter's woman was alone on the beach holding a knife in her hand.

NINE

Ice

The blizzard obscured the sunrise at Regina base.

The storm blew down over the steadily thickening layers of ice covering the Northwest Territories to strike hard at the empty towns and the few humans remaining in Alberta and Saskatchewan; it spilled over the leading edges of the piedmont glacier at Lloydminster and Edmonton and dumped unmeasured decimeters of new snow into the deserted streets of Saskatoon. There was no human eye to witness the collapse of another roof or the fall of another building. On the runway outside the base a great drift had piled up between the aircraft and the nearest wall, smothering the underbelly of the fuselage and totally obscuring the doors facing the storm. Shopwindows were opaque. The outside temperature hovered uncertainly at minus forty degrees.

Fisher Yann Highsmith opened hurtful eyes and found himself slumped over Jeanmarie's workbench in the ready room, the fingers of one hand curled around a marking pencil. There seemed to be new markings on the map under his hands, but he was entirely unable to focus on them.

He squinted at the window and realized dawn had come—for whatever dawn was worth—but the window was thickly coated with frozen snow, denying him the visibility. The chair refused to move with him when he leaned back and he cracked his bony shoulders before realizing he was sitting in Jeanmarie's chair, not his own comfortable throne stuffed wtih ostrich feathers. Highsmith shut his eyes in a tight grimace, scrubbed his face with dry hands, and then opened his eyes again. The sting in them would not go away. He guessed he'd had three or four hours' sleep.

Highsmith stood up, retrieved his operations map, and stepped sideways a few paces to sit down in his own chair. That felt better and he toyed with the idea of going back to sleep. His bleary eyes focused on the pictophone and the next thought changed his mind about sleeping. He reached out and punched the numbered buttons for the tower.

"Sergeant?"

The gloomy face of a corporal stared back at him from the screen. "Hello, Fisherman. The sergeant ain't here—he turned in. I guess I'm officer of the watch."

"What's the word on Search One, officer of the watch? I expected them back this morning."

"They ain't coming in, Fisherman. Not now, they ain't. Search One is holed up in Regina. They can't move, this storm has got them pinned down. Wolves, too."

"Not at all?"

"Not until the storm lets up."

"They've got my canoe out there!"

"Maybe they'll use that for firewood," the corporal said helpfully.

"They damn well better not! Are they safe?"

"Well, yes and no. They're sitting out the storm in the old post office, so I guess they'll be all right so long as they stay there. The roof is still up." He peered down at the recon man. "But do you know what, Fisherman? They got company! The radio man told me there's a wolf pack in the post office—just living right in there with them. The pack followed them into the place."

"But are the men *safe*?"

"Sure they are, for now. The team is holed up in the postmaster's office with their sled heater, and the wolves are out in the mail room. Somebody left the loading doors open when they abandoned, and the wolves took over the mail room. The postmaster will hear about *that*."

Highsmith blinked at the information but ignored the incongruity; he was too tired to sort it out. There was something else he should ask, something hanging at the back of his mind, but it wouldn't come into focus.

The corporal waited for him.

When it finally came, he almost shouted at the phone. "Hey! *We're* supposed to have company. Harley ordered up a hospital unit and a couple of nurses!"

The corporal jerked a thumb at the unfriendly sky. "It's up there, *they* are up there—they've been hanging up there for an hour or so, Fisherman. They can't come down on account of this blizzard, the pilot said. No guts, I said." He seemed genuinely regretful.

"Harley will be mad! He wants that unit."

"I want them nurses. I haven't seen a woman for *years*, almost."

"Jeanmarie is a woman."

"That ain't what I meant, Fisherman. Jeanmarie is a librarian and librarians don't . . . they don't . . . well, they'd rather go read a *book*."

"I didn't know that," Highsmith exclaimed.

"Take my word for it, Fisherman. I'm an expert."

Highsmith rocked in his cushy chair musing on the new found knowledge—if it was knowledge rather than hearsay. He wondered where the corporal had gained his wisdom.

"I'm going to think about that."

The officer of the watch said, "Sure," and cleared the channel. The jot of light faded from the center.

Highsmith stared at the dead screen, listening intently. The ready room was unusually silent; a sound was missing and he turned the chair around to search the room, seeking the point of absence. The snoring was absent, and Highsmith stared at the corner. The pilot was awake and on the edge of his cot, dully contemplating the floor. He seemed to be looking for his boots, which were just beyond his stockinged feet. The man had a surly air about him as though he suffered from lack of sleep.

Highsmith said: "Good morning."

"Go jump," the pilot muttered, and then he grunted with an inner satisfaction as he discovered the boots.

Highsmith said: "I've got news for you. Do you want it now, or after a hearty breakfast? You might be in a better mood after breakfast."

The pilot stopped his bending, reaching motion and let a hand rest atop the first boot. From that position he swiveled his head to stare at Highsmith, measuring him and his statement and seeking hidden meanings. After a long and searching scrutiny he let his gaze wander along the workbench behind the recon man and come to rest on the polygon weapon. The artifact fell under the same searching study. In very slow motion the pilot picked up the first boot and came to his feet.

"What did you do?"

"I think you should have breakfast while it's hot," Highsmith told him. "They shipped in eggs this week."

"What did you *do* to my ship?"

Highsmith said quickly: "Now take it easy. It's just a little hole. The shop crew can fix it in no time. I'm sure they have plenty of spare parts around."

A rising bellow shook the room. "*What* did you do to that ship? Did you *damage* my ship?"

Again: "It's just a little hole in the tail piece. I think you call it the elevator, the little flap that goes up and down. Not very much, really. I was making some tests out there and I didn't realize—"

Highsmith broke off and dodged the thrown boot. He thought the pilot was coming after him, and then he thought the man intended to run outside barefooted—or at least in his stocking feet, which was next to barefooted. The pilot had lunged at him with murder in his eyes, then turned in midstride and sped for the door. He vanished through it on a blind run, cursing Highsmith and his parents in a thundering voice that must have carried to the kitchen.

Highsmith didn't think it was fair to bring his parents into the discussion, but he bounded out of his chair and ran after the pilot to stop him, to prevent him from leaving the building without his boots or warm clothing. He realized the man wasn't thinking clearly. Somewhere up ahead, around a turn of the corridor, he heard a heavy crash as the running pilot hit the door and rebounded. A second and equally jarring thud followed. Highsmith slowed to a halt and craned his head to look around the corner.

The angry pilot was banging and kicking at the door in a futile attempt to open it, and colorful obscenities which had begun at Highsmith's expense were now partly directed at the obstinate door. It could not be opened. It was one of the northwestern panels facing the storm and now was sealed fast by the accumulation of packed snow on the outside; it likely wouldn't be opened until the storm blew over and a crew went out the leeward door and worked their way around to it. The enraged pilot charged the obstacle another time and the resulting collision seemed to shake the walls. Someone shouted at him from the kitchen, and someone else stepped out of the mess hall to see what was happening. Doors opened along the corridor.

Fisher Highsmith thought it prudent to withdraw. He

walked quickly and quietly back to the ready room and closed *its* door without a sound. The cursing and pounding were still audible around the the the turn of the corridor.

From behind him a curious voice asked: "What's all the fuss down there, Fisherman?"

Highsmith turned with a guilty start and found the communications corporal looking at him on the screen. The man was bent forward with his nose almost touching the lens.

"It's just somebody trying to open the outside door, Corporal. The storm sealed it shut."

"Well now, he doesn't have to be so damned noisy about it," the corporal complained. "I thought the house was coming down—and if he wakes up the sergeant, oh boy, he's in for it!"

"I think somebody's out there with him now. They will talk him out of it." Highsmith stood with his back to his own door, listening to the rumbling noises beyond it.

"That idiot ought to know he can't go outside in this storm!" The corporal peered from the screen with indignation. "If he *has* to go outside, why don't he go around to the back door—the shop door?"

"I didn't ask him," Highsmith admitted. "Maybe the back door is blocked shut."

"No, it ain't. I checked. Some of the shop guys are running in and out, testing the sleds in case they have to go into town. That door is open all right. He'd better not wake up the sergeant."

"Have you heard anything more?"

"I heard plenty from Weather Central in Billings; it hasn't hit them yet, but they're expecting it any time now. They've put out snow warnings and citizen advisories. We've got us a first-class blizzard here, Fisherman. Those guys in Billings have been watching it, and they said we're in for it. I told them we already was."

"Is the hospital unit still upstairs?"

"Still up there, just buzzing around. The pilot was telling me about the bright sunshine up there."

Fisher Highsmith still had his back to the door, listening to the commotion down the corridor. It seemed to have lessened. Perhaps cooler heads were prevailing and the pilot was realizing the folly of going outside. The man would probably be difficult to live with for a few days.

The pictophone screen went dark.

Fisher Highsmith wandered out into the shop. A knot of men were clustered about two sleds at the back of the shop but he ignored their activities and turned his attention to the workbenches along the near wall.

The results of his labor rested there and he was rather proud of the work.

The reconstructed ravelin had been built up from the floor to the very edge of the bench, and Highsmith considered it a most satisfactory job. The two artifacts were almost the same height. The ravelin appeared to be neat and orderly to his professional eye, faithful to the never-seen original, and something old Seventeen would be proud to crouch behind. He keenly anticipated the day when Harley would permit the warrior to visit the shops and inspect his handiwork. With uncommonly good luck and a sure hand, Highsmith had even worked the keystone of sorts into the topmost tier: he had fitted in that one mud brick which contained the imprint of bird feet and a dropping. He thought *that* a masterful touch, and hoped Seventeen would appreciate it. The reconstructed ravelin was about a meter and a half in length, and about as high as a warrior's belly—a place for hiding, not fighting. It was a device for lying in wait, a place of ambush.

And it was failure: as much of a failure as its seventeenth-century counterpart.

A naked brick ravelin built on a hillside—on a drumlin or esker or moraine—was a feeble instrument of ambush, an exposed farce. It might deceive some wild game, those birds or animals suffering from restricted eyesight or having a poor sense of depth perception, but it would stand like a sore artifact to any other human having his wits about him. The mud wall, obviously artificial, would offer sharp contrast to the grass and chickweed surrounding it, beneath it, and behind it, but yet these ravelins were popular, to judge by the evidence— to judge by the debris coming down in several different locations. Future brickmasons built them with regularity while future warriors hid behind them and were killed with that same depressing regularity. They were failures even while they offered early concealment to those warriors hiding behind them, watching the approach of the enemy.

An idea occurred to Highsmith and he toyed with it for a while, wondering if it was valid. Consider the normal eyesight of warrior and enemy alike. Were they equal? Was one as sharp as the other? Or did the primitive warrior possess a superior range of vision, and he had learned by hard experience that the approaching enemy was unable to see his ravelin until the enemy was almost upon it—say, within easy striking range for the defender? Would that lead the warrior to believe his naked mud bricks were enough, lead him to think *he* always had the advantage over a handicapped opponent?

Highsmith dropped to his knees to examine again the face of the structure for traces of camouflage. There were none. The polygon weapon would have probably burned away any weeds or sticks or skins used for the purpose, but even so there should be traces of camouflage—tiny clues pointing to the existence of it. None. He could only conclude that the blue-eyed warriors were woefully unprepared for matching wits and skills with the invading enemy, even granting them for the moment a superior vision. That range of vision may have deceived them, may have led them to think they were superior in other ways as well—to their regret.

The weapons offered hard proof of a superior force. The man in sick bay—and his sixteen dead brothers— fell by the numbers because they continued to rely on the mud walls for shields. Those ravelins might work well enough if they were used as blinds for stalking birds or small game, but they were useless against the well-equipped invaders coming up from the south to reclaim the new lands freed from the ice. The invaders carried fire in a deadly kind of box.

His gaze moved up to the newly reconstructed polygon on the bench. *That* had been a difficult thing to put together, even with a working model before him. He'd tried and failed to imagine the mental processes of an inventor bent on fitting a weapon into a polygon casing. Why that shape? Why not a box or a ball or a rectangle or a length of piping? What kind of genius had played with a polygon?

Scores of the hard rubbery shards—which were not really rubber at all—had been cemented together to form the rebuilt weapon, and a weight had been set into the bottom to lend the proper feel and heft to the thing, but Highsmith was still disappointed with the finished product: it looked like something an apprentice archeologist had put together, an artifact built up from rubbish —a poor museum piece to be displayed with a printed apology. The miserable reconstruction wouldn't fool Seventeen if it were put into his hands. He would likely grind it underfoot after the briefest examination, or hurl it at the nearest target of opportunity—at Highsmith himself if he had presened it for the examination.

For several minutes last night Highsmith had toyed with the idea of taking apart his working model, of finding out for himself how and why the strange weapon worked. He was neither inventor nor engineer, much less a weapons expert, but he had a burning desire to *know* what made it go when it went. He wanted to know why it fired only when it was grounded. The weapon could not be used inside an aircraft in flight and that led him to suspect the invading enemy lacked aircraft; it couldn't be fired from a truck or horse-drawn wagon and so the invaders would have to leap to the ground for combat, exposing themselves to counterfire. It couldn't be used while standing on a chair, a table, or a staircase; it was a useless weapon when fighting on housetops or castle battlements unless those structures had numerous water pipes or ground wires placed at convenient points —and *that* was a silly arrangement. He guessed the invaders simply fell down onto their stomachs and blazed away at Seventeen and his brothers.

The other mystery of the weapon was the nature of the charge, and the source of that charge. What substance buried in the polygon burned a man and propelled him and his mud bricks out of time—what propelled him back into Highsmith's year? Harley insisted on radiation, some kind of radiation, and the prospect of finding a radioactive nugget in the center of the polygon stopped Highsmith's hand. He abandoned the idea of taking apart his working model even while he continued to speculate on the weapon.

He wondered if the inventor—and the people who used the gun—knew what they were doing to their victims? The hideous burning and killing was obvious, but where did they believe the victims were going when they disappeared? The cleansing of a battlefield was equally obvious, but where did the graves detail think they were dumping their bodies? Did they really *know* they were shoveling them backward into someone else's century, or were they content that the field was clean and never mind the niggling questions? For that matter, were they aware at all that their victims were falling *here*, or in other times? Perhaps they thought the weapon merely disintegrated the victim, reduced him to dust.

After a lengthy comtemplation Highsmith decided that was the most likely answer, an acceptable solution: the genius didn't fully understand what he—or she— had invented. When the victims vanished it was assumed the weapon had disintegrated them, and someday the authorities would have to do something about air pollution. Given that answer, Highsmith hoped the invaders never discovered what they were actually doing to their victims. If they did, it would only be a matter of time— and a succession of other geniuses—before they improved upon the weapon and found a way to convert it to transportation. He didn't relish the idea of a pack of invading women with fire in their eyes—and their hands —descending on *him*.

Highsmith speculated on yet a third weapon—on the possible possessor of a third weapon.

At least two of the radiation guns had been taken from the invader, taken by force or by guile or simply lifted from the corpse of a loser. Two of the weapons were on the bench before him, but did a third exist somewhere on the snowfields? The first liberated weapon was the poorly reconstructed piece on the bench; some homeland defender had been carrying *that* when he was discovered and gunned down. A second stolen weapon was the undamaged working model that had come down on the ice shelf with old Seventeen—and Highsmith wanted to believe it had been in his possession when he fell. Thus far, two polygons accounted for.

But was there a third, still undiscovered? Were there a number of others now in the possession of the warriors, and the possibility that the teams might find *them* in the coming months? If two could be wrested from the enemy, why not more?

And didn't the defender *ever* fire at the invader?

No one had ever found a scrap of tailored cloth, a fragment of uniform or boot or helmet to suggest that an alien invader was on the scene; there were no shattered bits of an enemy vehicle, a wheel or the spoke of a wheel, a piece of armor, something from a field kitchen —nothing but two weapons and seventeen fallen men to suggest that an enemy existed. Highsmith wondered if the beaten warriors had ever learned how to use their stolen weapons before they themselves were knocked down by others like them. Had they ever been given time to learn the weapons had to be aimed and grounded to be fired? Or were those defenders so ignorant they could not learn the use of the polygon? No amount of practice with a Yakut bow would prepare a man to fight with the polygon, no amount of skill with knife or spear would help. They had to watch the gun being fired, and they had to realize the necessity of a good ground. Were they that intellingent?

Highsmith sighed and shrugged. The search teams kept turning up specimens like Seventeen; they had never yet found one of the hypothetical enemy.

The ready room was empty and hushed, and he was grateful for that. Perhaps the pilot was at breakfast. Highsmith was halfway across the room to his bench when the screen came to life and the corporal peered down at him again. The man was eating his breakfast on the job.

"I've been looking for you, Fisherman."

"Here I am."

"Guess what? We've got *more* company upstairs now."

"This place is getting crowded."

An agreeable nod. "Another craft circling around up there in the sunshine. That makes two of them."

"The bureaucrats!" Highsmith declared.

"That's who they are," the corporal said. "Flew all the way up from Washington South to inspect your ice man. I guess that makes you famous, or something. The bureaucrats are impressed. But they can't come down —the pilot is afraid to come down, so I guess they'll just have to hang there along with them nurses."

"Let 'em hang," Highsmith said. "Do them good."

Wistfully: "I wish the nurses could come down."

"You and Harley together. He'll raise hell when he learns the hospital is up there; he wants that hospital to keep the ice man alive."

"Maybe I'd better find him and tell him."

"Maybe you should. Anything more on Search One?"

"All the time—we're keeping the line open now. Same situation. They can't move out of the post office, but the wolves are starting to give them trouble. If *that* keeps up I'll have to rouse the sergeant."

"Why? Can't you send out the rescue team?"

The corporal seemed offended. "Me? Of course not. I'm not the security officer, I'm the officer of the watch."

"There's a difference?"

"Fisherman, don't you know anything about channels?"

"Excuse me," Highsmith said. "I'm not a military man, I don't know the channels."

"Well, just take my word for it. I'm an expert."

Highsmith nodded and remembered the last advice he'd recieved from this self-proclaimed expert. He didn't want to believe that polylibrarians would prefer to read a book. He entertained several warm notions about Jeanmarie and it would be a cruel blow to learn that she preferred a book to him; it would dash his hopes of asking her to go to Mexico with him—and Harley—when the base was closed.

The corporal said: "I'd better call Doc."

Highsmith waved him out and sat down in the plushy chair that some officer had left behind for him when the airfield was abandoned. His bony frame appreciated the gift. He stared sleepily at Jeanmarie's map, and hoped she wouldn't be upset when she discovered he'd drawn pictures on it.

They weren't doodles; he hadn't been doodling on the operations map. He thought of the additions as genuine reconstructions of recognized value, and as pertinent to the problem at hand as that ravelin in the shop. Highsmith had sketched in an inland sea as well as a number of eskers and drumlins, a map of things to come. Yesterday the map had reflected the current state of operations, yesterday the map had shown seven square sections marked off in red to pinpoint the most recent falls of debris—seven sites in three northern states. Yesterday there had been a ragged red line north of the base, reaching from the nearer slopes of the Rockies to the middle of Hudson Bay, telling the leading edges of the icefield. Now that was changed.

Highsmith had sketched in a lake, the new Lake Agassiz as he imagined it would be a few thousand years in the future when ice blocked the major rivers. It was more sea than lake, a vast body of water covering all of Manitoba, and spilling over into Saskatchewan, Ontario, North Dakota, and Minnesota. Cities as far west as Saskatoon, as far east as Kenora, and as far south as Fargo and Moorhead were under water. This base—and Regina, of course—were under the surface because an arm of the sea stretched southwest toward Montana. The shorelines were guesswork based on what Jeanmarie had told him, but they could be firmed with the arrival of the geological maps ordered from the agency. It seemed reasonable the new sea would replace the old one.

Superimposed on the seven squares Jeanmarie had put down to locate debris areas were his drumlins. One of them was actually in the sea and another was dangerously close to it, and although that was a worrisome thing it couldn't be helped with his present state of knowledge: mud bricks *had* fallen there, and Seventeen had tumbled from one of them. He had sketched in only a few dozen of the ice-carved hills but in reality there would be hundreds of them grouped in a given place. Highsmith had patterned the drumlins after those in Michigan and Wisconsin, the hundreds of elongated hills looking like huge wrinkles of earth crust from the air. They didn't always run from north to south because the ice seldom flowed in a true southerly direction; rather they seemed to radiate from a strong central point and could be found stretching to the southeast, the south, and the southwest. Many of the drumlins were two kilometers or more in length, none were shorter than two hectometers, and the largest of them were sixty meters high. They offered a distinct vantage point over the plains below, or over the glacial streams flowing between drumlins if the invading enemy came by water.

Sketching in the eskers was pure guesswork, and he was content with only a couple of them. Eskers could appear at any place where a melt-water river coursed under the ice, piling up a sand-and-gravel bed to be exposed when the ice was gone—a sandy hill snaking like the river before it across a piedmont plain. They were erratic and not nearly as numerous as drumlins or moraines. He didn't believe that eskers were built as high as drumlins —he'd have to check with Jeanmarie on that—but he knew them for long and winding hills; some of those in Maine were sixty kilometers in length and their elevation offered a splendid advantage over an adversary passing below.

All things considered, Highsmith was proud of his work. He was pleased with the drumlin now burying the town of Lloydminster, because Seventeen had fallen there from a height and he regarded the battered warrior as *his* find; he was pleased that his imagination had led him to sketch in an arm of Lake Agassiz covering Regina and the base, because evidence hinted that Eighteen was coming there. A map of the future *should* look like that: an inland sea there, surrounded by drumlins there, there, and there, and an imaginary esker or two to round out the whole. Fallen debris dictated the features of the map; ancient history and a canoe fragment dictated the placement of the sea—not to mention a fall of fish. Those fish were entitled to their place in history.

He hoped Jeanmarie wouldn't be annoyed with his work. A map of the future rather appealed to him.

Fisher Highsmith wasn't aware that he had fallen asleep over his wondrous map of the future; he wasn't aware of his being asleep at all, for any length of time, until he opened his eyes over an expanse of plastic paper and found his nose resting on Manitoba in the middle of an inland sea. The red lines were blurred out of focus. Somewhere above him or behind him in the hazy world of the ready room Jeanmarie was repeating yessir, yessir, yessir, in dreary monotone. Highsmith thought that was a rather strange behavior on her part, and raised his head to look.

She pushed it down again at once. His nose smudged the Lloydminster drumlin.

From a long distance away, from the back of the room or the doorway or the corridor beyond, the doctor was crying his anger. "I want that unit down here now! I want it! No excuses, I won't take excuses. Bring it down!"

Jeanmarie repeated yessir, yessir, yessir.

Highsmith rolled sideways across the map and slanted his eyes up at the woman. He was careful not to lift his head. Jeanmarie was talking to someone on the phone above him, talking over him, and if he tried to sit erect he would come between her and the image on the screen. He held still, quite content to watch her face for the moment. Her manner of speaking betrayed the hurt to her jaw.

Something in the conversation passing over his head caught his attention, and he concentrated on the words.

A voice said: "We are returning to Washington South. Our pilot advises us that if we remain here another five hours and still cannot land, we will be in a difficult position with respect to fuel capacities. Weather Central in Billings believes this blizzard will not blow itself out for several days; it is a major storm and only the first of many to come."

"Yes, sir."

The voice said: "You may alert your personnel and make whatever preparations are necessary for abandonment, but do not begin the actual move until you recieve a written directive from the agency. In the meanwhile, notify the resident physician that his patient is to be flown out as soon as the weather permits. He will be advised of the loaction of the hospital prepared to receive him. I will inform the Director of these developments when I return to Washington South."

"Yes, sir."

"I believe the Director will agree with my judgment in these matters. This has become a critical area and your position will soon be untenable. Has your base commander dispatched a rescue party to assist those men in Regina?"

"No, sir."

"Order it done at once."

"Yes, sir."

Fisher Highsmith nodded his agreement. He was eager to get his hands on the canoe fragment.

The voice said: "Advise the agency when they are safely returned to your base. I will issue an order in writing to discontinue the search teams in this area; they are quite useless now. The order will be subject to review by the Director, but I think you may expect it in a day or two. Perhaps it will be transmitted to you along with the directivé of abandonment."

"Yes, sir."

"We are leaving now. We regret not being able to drop down for a visit, polylibrarian."

"Thank you, sir."

"Goodbye and good luck."

"Thank you, sir."

A chime signaled the disconnection.

Harley yelled: "I want that unit down here *now*!"

Highsmith came up off the map with alacrity, at the cost of a knee banged against a bench support. "Jeanmarie, are we breaking up?"

"Yes, sir." She stepped back a pace away from the phone. "This base will be closed and the personnel relocated to other installations. I was speaking to the Assistant Director. He is convinced the nearness of glaciation has rendered this area useless, and will recommend the base be closed." In an afterthought, she said: "He appeared very annoyed by the storm; he wanted to see the live recovery."

Highsmith felt dismay. "Relocated!"

She understood his meaning, his unspoken thought. "In past practice, the personnel of a closed station are distributed among several other stations."

"How long do we have? Six months?"

"Past practice suggests no more than two months."

"I'll quit—I'll resign! I'll go to Mexico with Harley." Highsmith dropped his voice and peered around the woman, but the doctor wasn't in the room or the doorway. "Is the hospital unit coming down? We *need* that unit."

"The matter is undecided. The pilot is afraid to risk a landing, despite the urgency."

"Damn it—Harley will have a fit!"

"Yes, sir."

Irritably: "Stop saying 'Yes, sir' to me! I'm not that bureaucrat upstairs, and I'm not your superior. My name is Fisher Highsmith, or you could call me 'Hey, you.' "

She took another step away. "Yes, sir."

Highsmith bounded from the chair and reached out to take her arm. "I'm sorry, Jeanmarie. I really am." He tugged gently on the arm, pulling her close to him. "I apologize. But please stop saying that—I don't feel like a 'sir,'" He felt warm at this moment.

Jeanmarie said: "I should inform the doctor." But she didn't immediately move away from his hand.

They stood for a while in the softly lighted ready room, only looking at each other and contemplating the next move—if there was a next move. Highsmith wasn't certain he should risk one. He could hear the glacial winds beat against the wall behind him and whip over the roof, while somewhere nearby, perhaps in the back shop, a loose door rattled under the onslaught. The driving snow had never stopped and in their little silence the fury of the storm was magnified. He realized he was very near to blurting out his secret thoughts.

The pictophone called for attention.

Highsmith spun around and looked again at the gloomy face of the corporal in the tower. The man was unhappy.

"You choose the damnedest times!" Highsmith cried.

"The first aircraft is gone, Fisherman, and the other one wants to." The corporal's melancholy gaze went to Jeanmarie and then to the hand resting on her arm. "Those nurses might not come down here."

"We have to hold them, Corporal. Tell them!"

"I just talked to the pilot. He's ready to kiss me good-bye—you know what I mean—and he's already told me what I can do with this here storm."

"Don't let him go. Make him stay!"

"He's the boss, Fisherman. It's his decision."

Highsmith let go of the polylib with reluctance and rammed his hands into his pockets. "I think we've lost all the way around, Corporal." He could guess the pilot's pungent words.

Again the gloomy nod. "I guess so." He stared once more at the polylibrarian and seemed to sigh. "Yup." The man's image wavered and the screen went dark.

Jeanmarie said: "I must inform the doctor now."

"Want me to do it?" Highsmith knew the warm tender spell was broken; it couldn't be recaptured now.

She shook her head and turned away. "It is my task."

When she was gone from the room Highsmith went to the bench and just stood there, suddenly at loose ends. He inspected the map of the future without real interest and looked at the many drumlins drawn over the seven red squares. His absent gaze roamed the shorelines of the future sea. Taking up the marker, he made an X over the map marker's circle representing Regina and then lettered a notation beside it: "canoe fragment." The impulse to add "fish and stones" was put aside. Charles Fort could look after the fish and stones: that was his province.

The rattling door nagged at his attention and he quit the room to look into the shops. There it was, at the rear: one of the double doors had been left ajar by the shop crew running in and out. Two sleds were parked at the doors, ready to be taken outside. Highsmith pulled the door tight and kicked at the snow that had blown in through the crack. Snow in the shops. These back rooms were some degrees colder than their living quarters and the snow was not quick to melt. *That* was clearly a portent of things to come. He supposed that in only a few years the roof would come down and the elements would claim these habitations, all the rooms would be filled with snow dumped in by never-ending blizzards; in only a few years the wolves would be living in the shops if the last man neglected to close the door. And in a century—perhaps more, perhaps less—the glacier would grind it all under. Dismal prospect.

In the following moment, a brilliant moment, he realized that he didn't give a damn. He just didn't give a damn about any of it. The wolves could take it.

The discovery elated him.

Fisher Highsmith suddenly knew what he would do when the base was closed down, and that added to the elation. A loud whoop announced his decision to the empty shop.

He would pack up his work and ship it down to Washington South, ship everything—the rebuilt ravelin, the reconstructed weapon and the working model, the future map, the canoe fragment, all the unsorted debris on the bench, perhaps even the fish and stones if they were recovered, *all* of it—and pack it off to the sunny South as playthings for bureaucrats. And *then* he would dictate a report, a very thorough report, and dump it on the bureaucracy for their edification. He would dictate his ideas, his theory, his model for the future world, and shove it in their faces. Or perhaps he would offer the same suggestion the pilot had made the corporal in the tower.

And when he had delivered the lot they could do just any damned thing they wanted with it—he wouldn't care, because his resignation would go forward with the shipment. He would be on his way to Mexico with Harley, and with Jeanmarie if she could be persuaded. Especially with Jeanmarie. That was his elation.

Fisher Highsmith left the shop on the run to seek out the doctor and the polylib. They would be together in sick bay and they should be the first to know of the plans he'd made for the three of them. He ran down the corridor.

Highsmith unceremoniously shoved through the door into sick bay and yelled: "Hey! I've decided to—"

Jeanmarie put up a quick hand to hush him. She was beside the doctor at the warrior's bed.

Harley straightened up when Highsmith burst through the door and methodically removed his stethoscope, raising a fist to hurl it across the room. Jeanmarie grabbed the instrument from his hand.

Highsmith looked on in astonishment. "Is he dead?"

Harley turned on him. "Do you have some of that stuff, that liquid, that . . . ?" He appealed to the woman for assistance.

"Bourbon," Jeanmarie said.

"Do you have some of that bourbon for me? Do you?"

"Yes." Highsmith stared at him and then at the patient. "Yes, I've got some. Harley, is he dead?"

"He should be!" the doctor snapped. "He's so far gone he *should* be dead. He *will* be, in a short while." A commanding finger was pointed at Highsmith. "Go get that bourbon, get it! And bring me that polygon gun you have. If that pilot doesn't come down *now* we're going to shoot him down. We are!"

TEN

Iron

He had been a slave since early childhood.

He could remember a time in the dim long ago when he was not a slave, but the concepts of freedom and slavery weren't all that clear-cut. Freedom was when he and his mother and father lived in their own house, and his father worked outside all day; slavery was when he and his mother and father lived in a larger house with many other people, and all of them worked all day. If there was a greater difference it escaped him.

His memory of that early childhood was sketchy; only the exciting and impressive events remained to him. He could recall that he had been very young when the soldiers came to their house and made everyone get out of it before they burned it to the ground. The fire had been impressive. He had played in the house in cold weather and out of it in warm weather for as long as he could remember; there had been only two rooms in the house but he clearly recalled both of them, and when it burned he realized the rooms were lost forever: his father would not build them again.

He couldn't ever remember having a sister, although his mother often said he had one. *That* was a puzzling blank spot in his memory. His mother insisted that he once had a younger sister but that the girl had died after the burning of the house; his mother said the soldiers had gathered them all up after the fire and marched them to the town where everybody lived, but his sister had not survived the march. She had died on the third day after the burning and had been buried on the prairie. He could not recall that, or her, but he remembered the walk across the prairie; it was the first time he had ever been so far from home and it had left a lasting impression. He walked and sometimes ran, making a game of running away from his father and mother and then sitting down to wait until they caught up to him. Some of the soldiers played with him and some of them laughed at him, but they would never let him eat with them. When everybody stopped to eat on that long journey the soldiers always sent him back to his parents and made him eat with them.

The town was an astonishing place. The houses were larger than his own burned house, so much larger that he couldn't guess at the number of rooms in them; and there were so many people in the town he didn't believe there were enough houses to hold them all. It was a big, noisy, bustling place that left an indelible impression on his mind. The town belonged to the soldiers.

The soldiers took them to one of the very largest houses in the town and told them to go inside; he'd been pleased at the magnificent size of the place and pleased that it had been given to his mother and father because it seemed to be the biggest house in the world. The house had a very high fence around it and one of the soldiers had unlocked a gate to let them go in; he remembered that woman laughing and swatting him on the bottom as he ran through the gate. She locked it behind them. Disappointment came when he discovered the house was not to be theirs alone: a great number of people were already living there, people like his mother and father and many children like himself. The house was actually crowded with them and despite its size it had only three rooms. There was a smaller room at one end for his father and himself to go, and another room like it at the other end for his mother and the other women to go, while between the two was one tremendously long room where all of them lived and slept and ate. He remembered the straw on the floor and how sticky it was to sleep on. His mother cried at night.

He grew up in that house, and in others like it.

Sometimes he lived in smaller houses with only a few people like himself and sometimes he was moved back to the big house again where his mother and father lived, but there were times when he was transferred to other large houses like that first one where strangers lived. It really didn't make much difference. All the houses, big and small, had tall fences around them, and a gate that was always kept locked until he passed through.

When he grew older he discovered a subtle change in attitude on the part of the soldiers who unlocked the gates and those who went with them to the fields to oversee the work. He had grown taller and become much stronger than any of the soldiers, but that wasn't to be remarked because almost all the men who lived in the houses were the same. Like those others, he stood tall enough to look down into the faces of the soldiers when they talked, and like those others, he was called upon to do the heavy work the soldiers couldn't manage. The change became apparent when they began talking about him, talking about his strength and his ability to do this or that chore, and talking about the way his clothes fit him; they seemed to find some secret amusement in the way his pants fit. The change became pronounced on the day that two of the soldiers unlocked the gate and took him to the fields alone. That memory was as impressive as the firing of his father's house.

The same thing happened many times after that, always with the same two soldiers. They repeatedly warned him to silence and threatened to send him away if he spoke of the matter, but in return for his ready co-operation and his silence they always brought him extra food and something to drink later when he was exhausted.

During a winter when he was as tall and husky as he would ever be, he was moved to a small house behind a barracks, a new place where he'd never lived before.

There were a number of young males in the house with him, all of them serving the barracks, and all had been castrated to avoid the embarrassment of a pregnancy. His protectress—the tall dark-haired woman with knife scars on her arms, who claimed first rights to him—told him that she and her partner had bought him from the officer of the holdings. The explanation had been confusing because he'd grown up believing he was owned by the government, which was in another town he'd never seen, and it was difficult now to understand how one soldier could buy him from another. His protectress said that the officer of the holdings was in charge of all slaves and was responsible for them, but if a person wanted a particular male she could strike a deal with the officer. In a larger sense he still belonged to the government and always would—he was property—but in the here and now he was the chattel of the partners and subject to their command; he would remain with them until he was sold to another, or returned to the slave houses.

He lived in the house behind the barracks for a long while—until the journey began—serving first the tall soldier and then the light-haired one. The food was much better than he'd had before, and sometimes they would let him drink the beer all the soldiers drank.

There was an excitement in the town in the spring of one year, when preparations were made for a journey.

A motorwagon was brought out of the sheds and made ready. He was one of a gang of slaves who scrubbed out the interior of the big hauler and then stocked it with provisions, tools, clothing, medicines, and weapons brought from storage; he was one of the gang who were permitted to handle swords and axes because they were trusties, but his two protectresses brought down a locked box of quarterguns and stored it in the wagon because it was forbidden a slave to touch one. He knew how to fire a quartergun; he'd seen them fired often enough and had seen what happened to the animal or human victims before them, and he was confident that he could do as well if given the chance. He never understood why a soldier had to put them on the ground to make them work, but he knew they always fired that way.

When the hauler was full they made ready to go.

He noted that all the travelers were young, master and slave alike. More than half of all the soldiers in the town were making the trip, leaving behind only a caretaker force; the number of male and female slaves taken along would surely empty one of the large houses. He and some of the other males from the barracks service carried axes on their backs for chopping firewood, while those who were not so trusted would carry the loads they chopped. They would live off the land as they moved, reserving the provisions in the hauler for the lean days. The light-haired protectress told him they would be gone nearly all the summer, and at the end of the journey she would show him a great sea so vast the shore on the other side could not be seen. She said it was as cold as the ice in winter.

They left the town one morning at daybreak with the slaves walking in their place behind the heavy hauler. A road he knew well wound between the grain fields he knew equally well, and then in a short time they were out on the open prairies and that one particular memory of his boyhood came back to him. He remembered again the running game he played with his mother and father, and he thought he remembered the different smell of the prairie. It was a fresh and delightful smell after the closeness of the town, and here the wind dispersed the heavy perfumes the soldiers wore to let the new—or the long-forgotten—odors come in on him. They traveled the prairie for days without end, now and again stopping by a timber to make camp when firewood was needed. It was a pleasurable adventure.

After a while he discovered he could spot game before the soldiers did, and it pleased him to know that he was better than they were; there were many things he could do that they could not, but until now he hadn't realized his eyesight was superior to theirs. He didn't know what the animals were, didn't know their names, but he would find them by ones and twos grazing on a distant plain or squatting on a hill and watching the column pass. Often the soldiers never saw the game at all, and would march blindly by without realizing their nearness.

The forest astonished him.

It was so long from one horizon to the other that *he* couldn't see the ends of it, and so dense that the troop needed many days to get through it. It was a place rich in new and delightful odors, and a place of welcome coolness after the long journey under the summer sun. Never in his life had he seen so large a timber and it was a delight to walk through, even though he and the other males were kept busy chopping a road for the hauler. The motorwagon would find itself free to roll only a short distance through the trees, and then be forced to stop and wait until a way was cleared for it. The driver sitting atop the wagon would shout at them until the obstacle came down. In all, he thought it had taken them ten days to work their slow way through the forest and find the prairie again on the other side. The wagon driver was glad to leave the forest behind, but he was not; given his choice, he would be content to live the rest of his life in the place.

One day after leaving the forest shade he learned a new shock. There were men in the world who were *not* slaves, men who ran free and carried weapons in their hands.

Two men followed them out of the forest.

Until now he hadn't believed in free men, hadn't believed such men existed, because he'd never seen one. His mother and father had often told him *they* once were free, but he'd been skeptical because the burning of his father's house had meant only that they changed their place of living. The other old people in the slave houses had told much the same story but he hadn't believed them either—not fully believed them. *Now* he did, after the initial shock of discovery. He discovered the two free men following their trail, found them easily despite the distance, but he kept silent and waited to see what the men would do when they caught up to the column.

Later in the day there was trouble somewhere ahead and the entire company came to a halt in a long valley between hills. He heard cries and the shrilling of whistles at the front and knew the soldiers had stumbled into a danger. From his vantage point at a rear corner of the hauler he watched soldiers climb one of the hills and fire their quarterguns at something down the other side; after a while they came back down this side of the hill carrying two of their number and put the burdens on the ground beside a small pond. He and three other males were sent forward with spades to dig graves and bury the soldiers. He recognized one of the dead; she had lived in the barracks he served. The second was a stranger from another house.

They moved on toward the sea.

The far-stretching sea was truly startling and as impressive as the forest had been, the one as enormous as the other, and with but one exception the sea was all that his protectress had promised it would be. The waters *were* icy to the touch and they *did* reach out to incredible distances, but he saw another shoreline. He knew without asking that his protectress couldn't see it, but between him and the far horizon was a long, low white line that could only be another shore like the one he was standing on. A few trees grew there, and he thought he saw a fallen tree lying in the water. The air was clean and sharp and, although he dared not say so, he found it better than the heavy perfume his protectress was wearing.

There was more trouble that night.

As always, he was among the gang of trusties who helped the soldiers string two circles of trip wires about the camp for night security; they had been bothered by night-roaming animals since leaving town in the spring, and it had always been the practice to lay wires around camp when slaves were present. When the security net was in place and tested, his two protectresses took him along to their sentry post behind the camp. He ate with them and drank some of the beer which had been doled out of the hauler to mark the end of their journey. Afterward he lay in the grass with the light-haired woman for her comfort.

He was alone when trouble came. His two soldiers were a short distance away patrolling the wire when the free men from the forest crept in from the darkness. The slave rested on his belly on the bed of grass and smelled them, sniffed the unwashed odor of them, and wondered when the sentries would discover them. He was surprised they had crossed the outer barrier without tripping it and he wished now he could find them in the darkness—wished he could actually see them to know how close they were. They would soon be discovered and taken into custody.

The searchlight atop the big hauler came on, and the slave knew that they or some small animal had blundered into a wire. He flattened himself in the grass and waited it out, knowing the light would travel the entire length of the encircling wire and knowing his protectresses did *not* want him to be seen from the wagon. Taking a man on sentry duty would bring a reprimand. The light reached the sentries and stopped. The light-haired woman turned to face the hauler and wave a security signal, and then both watched the beam run back along the wire toward its end at the shore. They saw him hiding in the grass as it passed over his head, but gave no sign. When it was safely gone the slave turned his head to follow it, wanting to see the animal that had blundered in if the searchlight found it.

A small cry and a startled gasp behind him quickly brought him around again.

He lay on the grass bed paralyzed with fright until it was over, stunned beyond belief at what was happening. Never in his life had anyone fought a soldier except another soldier, and swift punishment always came to a man who touched one without invitation or permission. Until now, soldiers were inviolate. His two protectresses were down but he was too frightened to move, to utter a cry or touch the wire that would bring back the searchlight.

When it was over and the men from the forest had gone he crept toward the sentries and found them dead with their necks broken and their uniforms stripped away. His utter fright was doubled. He put out a finger to touch the wire and bring the searchlight, but then hesitated for another fear: *he* would be found here with the sentries; *he* might be blamed for their deaths. A panic choked him.

In the following moment the silence of the night was rudely shattered. A piercing scream came from a soldier down on the beach, and another whistled a warning; there was a shouting turmoil in the camp and the searchlight blazed out again to find a group of struggling people at the water's edge. He raised up to risk a look. A man was there, *another* free man fighting with soldiers. While he watched the man broke free and ran into the water to push away from shore, riding inside a floating tree. Soldiers dropped down to fire at him and the tree.

The slave dropped back to the ground to hide.

The men from the forest were coming again, running away from the camp and the sudden turmoil there, running from the trouble that another man like them had created. He huddled between the bodies of his protectresses to hide. The slave gaped in astonishment as they sped by only a short distance away—gaped in disbelief at the two females who ran from the camp with them. He knew them both, and knew they were supposed to be tied down for the night. The enormity of their act was as great as the killing of the sentries, and the fast accumulation of events numbed him. He raised up again to watch the females as they ran away, and realized they were going willingly. The free men led them into the darkness between the hills.

The slave reached out gingerly to touch the bodies of his protectresses and knew what whould happen next, what was certain to happen next. If blame was put on him for their deaths, he would be killed where he waited, and the three of them swept away together; but if he managed to escape the blame, he would still be punished for being found here with them, and then be sent back to the big houses. He was property. He turned in confusion to look down on the camp and the distant shore. Soldiers milled there, pulling someone out of the water. The other free man and his tree had vanished from the sea. Nearer at hand he could see some of the slaves moving about, although they should have been tied down with the two women.

A free man.

Overwhelming trepidation seized him and shook him, and he turned to run without a backward glance. Excitement blended with panic ran with him. He hurdled the trip wires and sped into the darkness between the hills, following the trail of the two free men and the slaves they'd taken with them. There was no outcry behind him and no pursuit.

Somewhere in the night he stumbled and fell, sprawling headlong over the graves he'd dug that same day. A hard object was crushed beneath him and he began a movement to brush it away, only to realize he was holding a quartergun. That too was prohibited to him but he kept it; he climbed to his feet and continued running with the weapon in hand, knowing that he would lose his life if he were found with it. He thought it was the gun taken from his protectress. When he had run an incredibly long distance, when he was winded and had to slow to a walk to keep from falling, he decided where he would go and where he would hide from the soldiers.

Given a choice, he would prefer to spend the rest of his life in the forest.

ELEVEN

Ice

Fisher Yann Highsmith was enveloped in a white whirl-blast. The polar temperature needled his body.

At only a dozen paces the doors he'd just passed through were gone from sight and the shop itself was as thoroughly lost as Lloydminster. The glacier could be a meter or two beyond the tip of his nose but he wouldn't know it until he slammed into the icy wall. Isolation was complete. Stinging sleet pelted his head and shoulders, forcing him to keep his back to the wind to protect his face; a furious wind eddied around him, driving snow into his face and threatening to topple his balance. Bitter cold penetrated his clothing.

When he could take the punishment no longer, Highsmith decided to give up his search and return to the warm comfort of the shops. The hospital craft wasn't here. It hadn't come down *here*, in the back lot behind the shops. The men of Search Two would have to find it somewhere on the runway, around on the other side.

The pilot had done a dumb thing.

Highsmith thought it was pretty heroic of that pilot to fight his way down through the blizzard, but then dumb to lose himself as soon as he landed. A *good* pilot would have put his craft down just outside òne door or the other, a *good* pilot wouldn't have people out hunting for him and his hospital gear. The man and his craft were lost.

Highsmith began walking backward, retracing his own steps and taking care to keep his backside to the sleet. Twelve paces exactly. That was as far as he'd gone in his search when he changed his mind. He counted off the twelve slogging paces taken due east from the shop door, and put out a hand to touch the door or the wall behind him. Wind and sleet were there. That was so surprising that he forgot himself and turned into the storm to thrust out both hands. No door, no comforting wall. He advanced another four paces with flailing arms, and the sleet iced over his goggles. Highsmith prudently stopped and turned his tail to the wind to consider the matter. He rubbed away the ice coating the goggles and looked at the belting snow. The shops had moved in his brief absence.

He'd passed through the door and advanced twelve paces into the back lot, and *then* he had retreated sixteen paces from the stopping place—from that place where he'd changed his mind. The logical move now was to go forward a total of sixteen paces, which would again bring him to his original stopping place, and *then* pace backward in a slightly different direction—always remembering to keep his back to the storm. *He* wasn't lost. The storm was blowing in from the northwest and if he always backed in that direction he would fetch up against the buildings sooner or later—or failing that, bump in to the disabled aircraft sitting around front on the runway—or failing that, bump in to the fence surrounding the field. The fence had to stop him if he missed the shops and the aircraft.

Highsmith struck off on the first of the sixteen paces forward. At the seventh step he collided with a man fastened to a rope and lost his balance. The man picked him up and thrust his face into Highsmith's hood, goggle to goggle. Highsmith recognized him.

Recognition was a figure of speech. The man wore a face mask that was wholly covered with frozen snow, while his goggles appeared to be cemented to the mask by the same process. Highsmith knew him to be the leader of Search Two by the homing device strapped to his chest and by the bulge of the earphones under his hood: the man was homing in on the bleeps being broadcast from the communications tower. There was no exchange of words between them; words were futile in that rushing wilderness of sleet and wind. The search leader seized both of Highsmith's hands and guided them to the rope tied around his waist—a lead line, strung out behind to each of the other men of the search party.

The second man on that rope came upon them suddenly and bumped into Highsmith before he could see and stop. The fellow made an impatient gesture.

Highsmith obediently hooked his fingers around the rope and fell into line as the leader moved off. He knew a quick alarm as he realized they were going in the wrong direction. They were moving away from the buildings at a forty-five-degree angle and Highsmith had the sinking feeling that the team was setting out on yet another sweep of the runway. He tried to call out a warning but the wind swept it away. Taking a firm purchase on the rope with his left hand, he raised the other to the leader's shoulder to catch his attention and banged his elbow on one of the double doors. The door slid past him as it was opened

Inside in the warmth and the relative hush of the shop, he could hear the bleeping tone that had brought them in. A small mountain of snow blew in with them.

"Well done!" he congratulated the team leader.

Twenty men crowded in behind him, all fastened to the lifeline. The lead man unstrapped the homing device from his chest and stripped off his goggles and face mask. His beard tumbled out in a bushy tangle.

"What in hell were *you* doing out there, Fisherman? Where did you think you were going?"

"I was searching the back lot for the aircraft."

"*We* searched the back lot. The ship isn't there."

"I didn't find it either," Highsmith said.

The leader unfastened his heavy parka and shrugged it off. He took a step closer to Highsmith and sniffed at his breath. "Why did you go out alone?"

"If you must know the truth," Highsmith retorted, "I was just strolling down to the river to watch the sunset. I wanted to watch the grass grow and listen to the birds singing in the trees for the last time. Didn't you hear the word? This base is being closed down."

"I heard the word. Fisherman, have you been skimming?"

"Of course not! I don't—"

The pictophone cut him off in the midst of denial. The officer of the watch had roused the security officer out of bed, and the sergeant's face looked into the shop.

"Did you find it?"

"No," two voices answered in unison. The team leader looked around at Highsmith. "Shut up and let *me* do the talking." He turned back to the phone. "The ship isn't out there, Sergeant."

The sergeant peered at them for a steady moment. "That pilot insists he's down."

"He's not on the runway and he's not on the back lot. Sergeant, we *searched*. We swept that runway going out and coming in again. He's just not there!"

"Did you search *off* the runway?"

"Sure we did! Sergeant, you know the size of a sweep with twenty men on a ropeline. I put the end man out at the fence and that left me with one foot on the runway —walking right at the edge of the runway. We went all the way around the perimeter. There isn't any craft out there except our own." The crew leader glanced at Highsmith and added a muttered comment: "And *that* one has a hole in it."

"The back lot?"

"We covered the back lot twice. No aircraft."

"Damned funny." The sergeant scowled down at them. "He dropped off my scanning screen, he's not up there in the sunshine faking it. He claims he rode my beam down, he claims he *is* down."

"Where?"

"He says he's on the ground, he says snow is piling up around him."

"I still say, where?"

"Damned funny," the sergeant said again.

"Are you still getting his signal?"

The face on the phone grimaced. "Do *you* want to listen to him?"

"No."

"I can't shut him up or shut him off," the sergeant complained. "He's too loud and too clear for comfort. Mister, he's down here somewhere."

"Not inside the fence, he isn't."

"Doc is in an uproar—he's got this base in an uproar. Doc wants that hospital gear."

"Send the doctor outside to find it."

Highsmith cleared his throat. "Did anyone look up on the roof?"

The sergeant stared at him for a solemn moment. "Bourbon again, Fisherman?"

"Take a look through your windows."

"My windows are iced over, all of them, and drifts are piled up as high as the tower eaves. I *can't* see out, Fisherman." The sergeant studied him a moment longer and moved his gaze to the crew leader standing alongside. "Maybe you'd better get a ladder, mister."

The crew leader muttered two words intended for Highsmith's ears alone as he reached down for his parka.

"I'm a trained scientist," Highsmtih retorted. "Scientists pride themselves on their fine minds."

Fisher Highsmith watched the parade down the ladder. He stood at the open door and craned his neck around it, unmindful of the swirling snow in his eagerness to greet the arrivals. The pilot came down first, glaring at those waiting in the shop and daring any one of them to offer a comment on his navigation. He helped the next person down the ladder but failed to offer similar assistance to the third, and Highsmith found out why when they had removed their protective clothing. He knew consternation. The two nurses were not the comely females he and the corporal had anticipated, not the possibly willing ladies from the warm southland, but rather one male and one female. Highsmith discovered the matched wedding bands on the ring fingers of each of them, and their behavior toward one another pointed up another fact: they hadn't been married very long. They were newlyweds.

The men of the search team brought down from the roof and into the shop what appeared to be a metric ton of equipment. The male nurse directed the unpacking of it, and after a parting kiss his young wife disappeared through the inner corridor door in search of the doctor and his hospital. The last man down brought in the ladder and shut the shop doors to block out the storm. It was shivery cold in the big room.

Fisher Highsmith looked around at the pictophone and found the faces of the sergeant and corporal crowding it cheek by jowl. They barely fitted onto the glass screen. The corporal fixed Highsmith with his doleful glance and shook his head in the manner of a man who has just witnessed the end of the world. His lips were a grim line. Next to him, the sergeant was staring at the male murse with something approaching disbelief.

Highsmith raised his hand in front of the phone to catch their attention. "Did my maps come in?"

"They're coming in now—dozens of them."

"What about Jeanmarie's book, the other half of her old history book?"

"That came in first. She's got it."

"All right." Highsmith nodded his satisfaction. "I'm coming up to get the maps. There's work to do."

But he waited a moment longer in the drafty shop watching the male nurse and the crew sort over the hospital equipment and start it along the corridor to the waiting doctor. Speaking over his head, the sergeant instructed the leader of Search Two to have his men fed as soon as they were finished with the task at hand and push off for Regina to assist the other team holed up there. The two teams were to return to base as soon as they were rested. The sergeant warned of the wolves and the need for weapons.

Highsmith studied the crew leader's expression and deemed it prudent to not mention his canoe fragment.

He left the shop and climbed the winding stairs to the

communications tower to get the maps coming in from Washington South. The facsimile printer was peeling off the last of them as he entered. The sergeant and his second in command had appropriated for themselves two comfortable chairs from belowstairs, and had set up a tea heater on a bench next to the printer.

Highsmith sat down in the corporal's unoccupied chair and stared with interest at the hot teapot. Immediately behind it was a small area of melted ice on a window, where the constant heat had created a tiny visual passageway to the outside world. Nothing but heaped snow was visible there. Neither of the men in the room caught the hint in his stare, and Highsmith reluctantly left off watching the teapot. He looked around at the opaque windows set into four walls. The storm had blocked the view on all sides by sleeting over the windows and the room itself was not warm enough to melt the glaze; it was almost chilly as the back shop. For an instant he had the impression of sitting in an igloo.

A small radio speaker at the sergeant's elbow carried the conversation of one of the men marooned in Regina.

"Ask him about my canoe," Highsmith said.

"Not again," the sergeant retorted. "He's damned tired hearing about that old canoe. Don't push it."

The corporal dropped the maps in Highsmith's lap.

"Where's the aircraft?" the Fisherman asked.

The corporal turned and put his index finger to a frigid pane of glass across the room. "Out there. The wingtip is two decimeters outside this window. Just *two*. That pilot cleared away a snowdrift coming down on us."

Highsmith considered the man's finger and the glazed window. A tiny melt spot began to appear where they touched. "That's pretty good flying," Highsmith said. "He didn't even crack it."

The ready room had returned to a quiet normalcy. The pilot was sleeping and snoring on his cot wedged into the corner and the two walls of that corner seemed to amplify the sounds; he slept in his clothing with his boots waiting beside him on the floor. Jeanmarie was seated at her bench next to his own, reading the remainder of the book that had come from the facsimile printer. She didn't look around as he entered, and he supposed the storm had masked the sound of the door. Only Harley was missing from the tableau. The room's one really bright light illuminated an empty place on the rug where Harley liked to sit and knit until the cold under the floor crept through and touched his backsides.

Fisher Highsmith put down his armload of maps and opened a storage drawer beneath the bench to determine how much of his bourbon Harley had consumed. Highsmith kept his liquid asset in a stoneware jug he'd found in an abandoned town in southern Ontario; he was of the opinion that stoneware added a certain taste to the smooth product. When Jeanmarie had first seen the artifact she'd said it resembled a toby jug, but that hadn't meant anything. He saw the shaped vessel as a jolly fat man whose hat was the stopper, and it pleased him that some townsman had left the jug behind for him and his licensed hobby.

Highsmith sipped with appreciation from his stoneware jug and examined the newly printed treasures.

A map supplied by the Geological Survey office was the most satisfactory of the lot: a map of the eastern and midwestern sections of North America, extending from New Brunswick westward to Saskatchewan and from the lower borders of the Northwest Territories southward to Kansas, Arkansas, and Tennessee. Perhaps three dozen states in all, a map of the last glacial age. It fascinated him.

Lake Agassiz was a dominant feature and it seemed even larger than Jeanmarie had described it: almost all of Manitoba and parts of five surrounding states were under water. Arms of water as large as gulfs crept westward into Saskatchewan at four places and another washed down into North and South Dakota; the main body of the lake inundated Ontario in two places, and spilled over into Minnesota. But Ontario was also wet on its other border. Far to the east of Agassiz another rising body of water emulated it, but on a smaller scale.

The St. Lawrence Sea opened from the Atlantic Ocean and flooded parts of Quebec, the eastern border of Ontario, New York, and Vermont, threatening to make an island of the New England states. The mapmaker suggested that the present Lake Ontario was all that remained of the sea except for the river of the same name which now occupied the center of the ancient seabed.

Highsmith was familiar with two of the three major rivers on the map, the old rivers of the icy years.

A preglacial Missouri flowed eastward out of Montana into North Dakota and then turned north into Manitoba; its waters helped feed Lake Agassiz when that body was formed. I later times—during the retreat of the ice sheets and slow death of Agassiz—the Warren River drained the lower portions of the great lake covering the Dakotas and dumped its melt into the upper Mississippi. The one prehistoric river new to him was the Teays, and he wondered what became of it. The map showed the Teays rising in Virginia and then flowing in a great northwesterly arc through West Virginia, Ohio, northern Indiana, and across the middle belt of Illinois to finally reach the Mississippi at or near St. Louis. It was as impressive as the Mississippi itself.

Forgetful that Jeanmarie was reading, he asked suddenly: "What happened to the Teays River?"

She hesitated only briefly, making a mental shift. "It was obliterated by the advance of the most recent ice sheets, primarily because the ice filled the riverbed with moraine. A large part of the river now flows underground through Ohio, Indiana, and Illinois."

"Underground?"

A quick nod. "Many cities and towns in those states have sunk wells into it to gain a fresh-water supply."

"It's still there," he marveled. "Fancy that."

"Are you ready to work on your maps?"

"I was waiting on you, Jeanmarie—I didn't want to interrupt." He showed her the Survey map. "This is the best one: prehistoric lakes, seas, rivers, ice sheets, moraines, drumlins, *everything*. I marked up your map yesterday but I want to transfer all that to this new one, and then add the new stuff." He gave her an anxious look. "You *are* finding new stuff?"

Jeanmarie smiled. "More than one can account for."

He peered over at her book. "Like what?"

"A variety of debris was found and recorded. There have been documented falls of stones, bricks, streams of water, ice chunks, slag, cinders, hot coals, pieces of glazed fragments resembling china, dust, fish, frogs, worms, snakes, vegetable matter, and what may have been a decomposed part of a human body."

Highsmith was thunderstruck. "What in the world is going on? Are they shooting at *everything* up there?"

"I prefer to leave that to you."

"Where did they find the body?"

"It was only a small part of a body and the person who examined the find, a lecturer at Dartmouth College, did not describe it as human flesh. The find was made at or near Amherst, Massachussetts, in August 1819, and was partially covered with a milled cloth. That created something of a stir."

"Amherst, Massachussetts!" Fisher Highsmith jabbed excitedly at his new map. "Massachussetts has drumlins —look at these drumlins!"

Jeanmarie said: "They were formed by the last glaciation. They may be eradicated by this one."

"But Massachussetts will get new ones! If they have them now they'll have them again, and some poor devil will be shot down there. *Was* shot down there, and fell in 1819. He was wearing a cloth garment when he was hit." Highsmith marked a red X on a drumlin. "Unknown defender of his homeland."

"Perhaps it was an animal."

He stared around at the woman. "Wearing milled cloth?"

"Horse blankets and dog sweaters."

"I never saw a horse blanket. I never *heard* of a horse blanket."

"They existed."

"I'll ask Harley about it," Highsmith mumbled. "What about the stone falls?"

"Trenton, New Jersey, in June 1884."

He studied his map. "Drumlins."

"Colby, Wisconsin, July 1917."

"Drumlins—Wisconsin is filled with drumlins."

"Hillsboro, Illinois, May 1883."

"A moraine on this map."

"Bismarck, North Dakota, May 1884."

"Moraine." He peered closely at the Survey map. "A large one—a terminal moraine. It diverted the old Missouri River, the one that emptied in Manitoba, and helped form the new one that exists now. A big moraine."

"Fort Ripley, Minnesota, January 1899."

"Oh, great! Fort Ripley is near an esker more than thirty meters long. That fits. One of the invaders blasted a pile of stones off the esker." He reached again for his stoneware jug. "Where did the bricks fall?"

"Richland, South Carolina. The date is not given."

Highsmith frowned and stopped the jug before it reached his lips. "That's off the map—that's too far south." He glanced around at the closed door. "I don't think old Seventeen roamed *that* far south."

Jeanmarie said: "Brickmaking is universal. Brick falls were also recorded in Great Britain and in Italy."

"They *are* shooting up the world!" He paused to sip from the jug and then looked back to the polylib. "Did you say worms? *Worms?*"

"Clifton, Indiana, and Lancaster, Pennsylvania. Both falls were recorded in February 1892."

A close examination of the map. "Lake Erie was partially drained by a river flowing across Indiana and Illinois when the other end of the lake was blocked by ice —a floodwater river. But Pennsylvania?" He looked again at his map. "The ice went down into Pennsylvania."

"After the ice, melt-water streams carried off the water into Chesapeake Bay."

"But that doesn't account for worms—who would fire at *worms?*" Highsmith gave the matter some thought and said at last: "I don't think I'll include worms in my report; Washington South isn't ready for worms. Give me a fish."

"Seymour, Indiana, August 1891."

"That same river flowing west from Lake Erie! And Search One found stones and fish falling in Regina." He bent forward over the bench. *"This* Lake Agassiz doesn't cover Regina, but the new lake—the third lake —will have to cover it to account for yesterday's fish. I think it was yesterday; I've lost track of time again." He sketched in an arm of Agassiz to flood the city and their base, as he'd done before on Jeanmarie's map, and then sat back to study his handiwork. He was pleased with his map of the future. "Fish, stones, and a canoe fragment. We're under water all right."

She said: "The stones are significant."

"I thought they were from the sea bottom."

"Stones were the first missiles. Slings and stones have been used from the beginning of Neolithic times, and some authorities believe they were employed in the late Paleolithic. They were first used as a means of killing game, and later incorporated into warfare."

Incredulously: "Slingshots?"

"Slings were a standard weapon of warfare in Europe and the Near East from the Bronze Age into the seventeenth century. Slingmen were superior to archers."

Highsmith frowned at that. "Difficult to believe. I believe *you*, Jeanmarie, but that's hard to believe."

"Their use in warfare is well documented, as is their proficiency. A bas-relief found in Nineveh portrays Assyrian sling troops stationed behind the archers while in battle formation; the slingmen fired over the heads of the archers but yet achieved the same or greater range. Those troops in the front lines of the opposing side were felled by stones and arrows. Several Greek and Roman armies also used slingmen to advantage."

He was thoughful. "What was the range?"

"One Roman military historian has indicated their archers usually achieved a range from one hundred and eighty to two hundred meters, using standard army equipment; the distance was considered satisfactory for that period. But at a later date another authority experimenting with slings noted that his men sometimes achieved a distance of two hundred and forty meters. That superior range would suggest why they were positioned behind the archers."

"I wish somebody would find a sling out there. Seventeen *should* have been using a sling—he's a Stone Age man, I guess." He stared at his stoneware jug. "Stones."

"Missiles. Archeologists have discovered hundreds and perhaps thousands of stones nested away in ammunition stores, although they were not immediately recognized as such. The Greeks and Romans later used clay and lead missiles for greater range and accuracy. Slings and stones are firmly established as weapons of warfare."

Highsmith waved a despairing hand over his map of the future. "We're getting stones, that fellow Fort got stones! But are we getting ammunition—or stones from the sea bottom, the river bottom?"

"That would be difficult to determine," Jeanmarie answered. "The ancient missiles were usually water-worn stones of a determined size, a particular size; those which were too small or too large were discarded because they would affect both the range and the accuracy. The Greeks in particular favored a standard weight and mass."

"I wish we could find a sling," he said again. "I wish Seventeen had *something* better than a Yakut bow."

"The Yakut was a lethal weapon in skilled hands."

"We haven't found an enemy with an arrow through his chest—*her* chest."

"The Canadian states haven't been thoroughly swept; these continual storms have defeated our purpose."

"Jeanmarie, I think you're agreeing with my theory. The knife that came down with Seventeen wasn't designed for throwing, was it?"

"No."

"It was designed for close-quarter work? Step in to an enemy, close with him, and thrust? Slice?"

"Yes."

"And they used the polygon for distance. Our man was up against a formidable enemy! I wish I knew how he got that knife and polygon, I wish I knew for sure whether he stole them from an enemy camp or fought for them. I like to think he fought for them—I like to think he whipped his enemy and walked off with the booty before somebody else caught him from behind. His condition suggests just that; it suggests that he just came in from Harley's lost battle—one of the lost battles."

"It may be a continuous warfare."

"You *are* agreeing." Highsmith wondered if he should offer her a pull from his jug. "Streams of water?"

"Streams of falling water ruined a house in or near Wellesley, Ontario, in July 1880. The water fell inside the house from a point immediately beneath the roof. The mysterious fall was never expalined."

"Ontario!" He examined the map. "Aha!"

"Pieces of ice also fell in Canada in July 1864. The town was given as Pontiac but the state or province was omitted. The place name may have been a misprint or a faulty translation for Ponteix."

"Where is Ponteix?"

"In southwestern Saskatchewan, not far from here."

"Aha!" he cried again, and fingered his map. "Under water! The western arm of Agassiz flows over Ponteix. The sea is falling down on us: water, ice, stones, fish, canoe. Jeanmarie, what if somebody up there is shooting at the water? Shooting at something *on* or *in* the water? What if somebody on shore is firing at somebody else paddling a dugout canoe on Lake Agassiz? Or firing from an elevation down into the lake? Wouldn't *we* get water, ice, stone, fish, and a canoe?"

"It is compatible with your theory."

"Was it Fort's theory?"

"It was not. He postulated another world above the sky, a physical world similar to our own but not a heavenly one. He suspected that debris was falling on the earth from that other world above in much the same manner that man-made debris cast into the oceans falls down on the marine life below. He liked to compare man to the schools of fish who bump into our debris as it is settling to the bottom. He sometimes thought we were receiving their garbage."

"Did his garbage float down—a lazy floating?"

"Some of it did, and was so observed."

"The idiot!" Highsmith exclaimed. "He had the key to the future and never realized it! Jeanmarie, his history book told the story of the lost battle centuries ago, but nobody realized it until now—until *me*."

Fisher Highsmith worked on his map most of the day, plotting the falls of stone, bricks, water, ice, cinders, slag, hot coals, glazed fragments resembling china, dust, fish, frogs, worms, snakes, and vegetable matter. Not all of the falls could be fitted onto the map because their geographical locations were beyond the three dozen states at his disposal, but he made a separate list of those distant falls for a later map. It was fascinating work. He was astonished by a report of ants falling on Manitoba, enormous ants the size of wasps, and again by another report noting a fall of lizards dropping in Montreal. He concluded that the fauna living in the Canadian states after the end of *this* ice age were truly startling.

The stoneware jug was sampled again. "Jeanmarie, what will the bureaucrats do if we find a gorilla or a dinosaur?"

When she turned to stare at him he twirled a little flag between thumb and forefinger, an imaginary flag.

The fall of decayed vegetable matter near London, Ontario, baffled him because it could not be fitted into his theory no matter how he twisted it. It was nonsense. What invader from the outside would shoot down a field of cabbages or onions or whatever? An estimated five hundred metric *tons* of decayed matter fell on London during a February snowstorm in 1868, and an examination under the microscope revealed the substance as a vegetable matter in advanced state of decomposition. The map showed him a conspicuous end moraine running along the northern shores of both Lake Erie and Lake Ontario, a distance away from the waterlines, but he wasn't at all certain that moraine or a new one like it could provide the necessary elevation near London. Of course, the history book didn't say *where* near London the substance fell.

In several instances the drumlins and eskers of the last ice sheet coincided with the recorded falls, opening the possibility they would not be erased by the new advance, but in other instances the map revealed nothing but open prairie and he was obliged to sketch in new elevations, as he'd done ealier on Jeanmarie's master map. Stones fell in Cumberland Falls, Kentucky, in April 1919; slag fell near Chicago in April 1879; cinders fell on an astonished farmer near Ottawa, Illinois, in January 1857; something described as "flakes of meat" fell on Olympian Springs, Kentucky, in March 1876. Highsmith marked the map. He was always delighted when the falls coincided with present-day elevations, be they molehills or mountains.

Sometime during the day—he wasn't sure just when—the rescue team left for the Regina post office. He heard the shop doors being opened and then the grating sounds of the sled runners moving across the concrete floor to meet the snow. He didn't envy the crew their trip into town. All of them worked for the same salary whatever his skill, but given his choice, he would rather earn the thirty dollars a month at a bench drawing maps of the future than slogging through snow searching for debris—or slogging into town to comfront the wolves. He wondered if he'd miss the job.

"Jeanmarie—?"

"Yes?"

"What will you do when the base is closed?"

"I haven't given it much thought. I suppose I will accept the assignment to another base."

"Don't you want to go to Mexico with me and Harley?"

"Has the doctor invited you?"

"Well, no—not yet."

"*Will* he go back to Mexico?"

"I don't know. He hasn't said anything yet—oh, he said once that he expected to stay up here with the ice, but I don't think he really meant it. He misses his wife. I think he'll go down to Mexico to be with his wife."

She asked: "Have you made a decision?"

"I made one yesterday, at least I *think* it was yesterday—it may have have been the day before. I decided to ship all this stuff down to Washington South, and send my resignation along with it. I'm quitting. And *then* I'll go to Mexico with you and Harley. I was going to tell you about it, and tell Harley; we should all go down there together and keep Harley company in his golden years."

The woman contemplated her hands resting on the open book before she spoke. "I had not considered Mexico, nor had I considered resigning. I can't speak for the doctor."

His spirits sagged with dismay. "You haven't?"

"There has been no reason to consider alternatives. I am content with my work."

"Jeanmarie, how long have we been on this base?"

"Nearly three weeks."

"Where did you come from? What was your last base?"

"Shawinigan, Quebec."

"How long were you there? Did they close it?"

"Shawinigan is closed now. I was there five months."

"And what before that?"

"None before that. It was my first assignment."

"Do you really want to stay here with the ice?"

She was looking at him, studying him and searching for a way to bring him to earth as gently as possible. "I want to stay in the north country, I'm fond of it. I was born here, Fisherman. I grew up in Shawinigan, and enlisted there. I want to stay until I am driven out."

"You and Harley," he said dully. The dream of old Mexico was already evaporating.

"I don't understand the reference."

"Harley is another northlander, he lived in Churchill until the ice drove *him* out. He had a horse."

"I can sympathize with him, and understand."

"Can't you sympathize with Mexico?"

"Not in the way you mean." She studied his face a moment longer and added: "I am sorry, Fisherman."

Highsmith nodded his understanding but said nothing more because he could think of no rational reply. He doubted that there could be a sane reply to a gentle refusal. He fixed his glance on the stoneware jug and kept it there a lengthy time, not trusting himself to look around at Jeanmarie. She was puzzling in many ways. She didn't seem too interested in men and she wasn't at all interested in going to Mexico. Mexico was a safe refuge from the ice, a snug haven for a few thousands years while the ice was grinding down everything else, but she wouldn't go there. They could always come back when it was over.

After a while he remembered what was in his jug and reached for it. The silence in the ready room was disturbed only by the pilot's snoring, and by Highsmith's quiet but appreciative comment: "Smooth."

Fisher Highsmith went along the corridor past the hospital room and thought to look in on Harley and his patient. He'd just left the mess hall, after picking over a poor supper; he was getting damned tired of spinach and, despite the cook's boasting, polar bear hadn't tasted all *that* good. Highsmith rated it only a notch or two above dog.

When he pushed open the hospital-room door he found Harley gone and the newlywed couple sitting close together on the spare bed, holding hands and each other. They looked at him as an interloper. Highsmith grinned to hide his sudden embarrassment and pretended a close interest in the patient. Seventeen appeared to be still among the living. His bed was now surrounded with hospital paraphernalia and a bottle of IV solution hung over him, feeding the liquid down a tube into a needle inserted into the one remaining arm. That arm was strapped to the bed. Highsmith gaped at the oxygen tent fitted over the warrior's head. The cardiogun rested nearby.

The male nurse asked: "You want something?"

"I just stopped by to see our patient," Highsmith said. He smiled at the young wife. "I have a special interest in him."

"Are you a relative?" the husband asked.

TWELVE

Iron

The stalking man huddled in the underbrush and warily watched the three women at the campfire. Their scent was strong and as strange as the cloth they wore to cover their bodies.

Two of the three were dangerous, two of the three carried knives in long pouches slung from their belts and carried black things in their hands that looked like stones or bricks; they were fighting women and not like those he'd grown up with, lived and mated with. He had seen the unsheathed blades working by daylight, had seen the sun glance off their gleaming sides the way it glanced off water to dazzle the eyes; he had watched the two with knives trap and cut down a small animal for their next meal, skinning and skewering it with a deftness that made him realize how poor his own knives were by comparison. Those two were skillful and the more dangerous to him.

When darkness fell and he edged nearer the women, closing in on them for the take, he discovered something more hanging from the tightly belted waists. The same two carried severed ears strung on a short cord, the dried and shrunken ears of fallen enemies. With *that* discovery, the man in the brush knew them. He'd never seen any of the women before, had never seen the place where they lived in great numbers, but he knew them; he'd grown to manhood hearing the tales of their savagery and he knew now he would have to kill to get what he wanted.

Each of them wore an unfamiliar cloth covering her body, a covering that didn't make sense to him because the summer heat was enouth to warm a body. If he'd found them far away, found them many, many days to the north where a great ice barrier stopped all passage, he would understand the need for cover; an unprotected man would shiver while standing next to the wall and would die if he was so foolish as to sleep beside it, but here in the open land where the sun was hot it was stupid to cover the body in such manner. It wasn't needed until the leaves dropped and the cold came. Two of the enemy had covered themselves in the same way: the two who carried the knives and the shrunken ears wore a cloth taken from the same animal and put together by the same person; their covering was the same color and fit, the same pattern and line, and they could have traded with each other without differences. Even the skin things they wore on their feet were exactly alike; the knives and the black bricklike objects in their hands were alike. Uniformity.

Only the third woman was different.

Her hair was markedly different to begin with and he studied the woman in fascinated attention. The hair was a lighter shade than he'd ever seen before; none of his own people had hair like that and none of them wore it in a knot on the top of the head. The pretty hair reminded him of the leaves on some trees that turned color when the end of summer was near. The cloth she wore over her body was equally different from the other two. There was not as much of it, leaving her arms and legs bare to the sun, and the color and fit of it were radically different from those of the two with knives; the lines of her body were easy to read and the skin things enclosing her feet were soft skins that appeared to have been taken from a different animal.

She carried no weapons. The stalker noted that with interest: she had no weapons and there were no ears hanging from her belt. The third woman carried *something* but he was certain they weren't weapons. She had a bundle of very thin skins or a substance resembling skins which were stiff and rolled up in her hand, and she had a small stick which made marks on the skins when they were opened. The three of them had spent most of the day walking about on the open prairie and then looking at the skins; they would walk entirely around a stand of timber and make a mark, or walk along a stream for a distance and make another mark, all the time talking among themselves and pointing off at nothing at all he could see. *She* wasn't dangerous to him.

She was for the taking.

At sundown the three made camp in a timber they had walked around and marked earlier in the afternoon, and there cooked the game they'd caught. Still more food was taken from a pouch one carried on her back and they drank from a vessel carried by another. He listened to their laughter as they ate. When the long shadows faded and the world turned a featureless gray the stalking man entered the timber after them and crouched in the underbrush to keep watch. He arranged his bone knives and his throwing stones on the ground beside him. The smell of cooking meat taunted his belly but he bided his time, waiting for the three to separate. He wanted those two shiny knives, the pouch and the food it contained, and the woman who was different.

The stalker watched them with a puzzled wonder.

Night had fallen, a darkness that was deeper inside the timber because the leafy canopy above blotted out the faint light of the summer sky. The stalker hugged the ground and feared to move because one of the women was looking toward him, looking out through the trees above him. She had turned around to let the fire warm her back and now he was pinned down. He dared not raise himself up again to look at the other two, yet it was their activities that puzzled him.

The other two were alone together in the poor light beyond the fire. Those two had separated from the third after their meal; they had walked hand in hand around the fire and a short distance away from it before settling to the ground. The fighting woman had unfastened her belt and let it fall and then the two of them stretched out on the ground with their bodies touching. It was not sleep: the fighting woman wrapped her arms around the third woman, *his* woman, and held her close while they talked and laughed and touched. The stalker watched them without understanding; he wanted to circle the timber and move in from the other side to see better, but before he could begin the move he was pinned down. The woman who had been left at the fire turned her back to it. She hitched her belt to move the knife pouch and the string of dangling ears and turned to stare out through the trees toward the open land.

After a long while that woman stood up and walked toward him. He knew a moment of panic and gripped his bone knives, believing she had at last discovered him. His own kind of women would have found him there long before—they would have seen him or smelled him when he crept into the brush at dusk. Incredibly, *this* woman did not find him. She went past him, passing so near he could have tossed a pebble at her feet, and he was astounded at her lack of skill. Her hands were empty. The stalking man darted a look at the fire and saw that the black brick was left behind.

The other two were still rolling and rocking on the ground beyond the fire. They laughed a lot and seemed not to notice the departure.

The stalking man slipped his knives into his skimpy breechcloth and picked up two of the throwing stones. He cast a final cautious glance at the two beyond the fire, and slipped through the brush after the woman who'd passed him. She had gone all the way through the timber to the open land outside. He stopped at the tree-line and scanned the prairie, thinking for a moment that he'd lost her because her shadow wasn't visible against the sky, but then she betrayed herself to him. He turned toward the smell of urine and hurled the first stone.

The woman toppled, thrashing awkwardly in the high grasses until the second stone—hurled from a point directly overhead—split her skull. The stalker tore the prized knife from its pouch and cut away the belt from her waist, hurling it and the severed ears far into the night. He ran his hands over her body, knowing wonder at the feel of the cloth but wanting booty. She had nothing but a magic talisman hanging around her throat and he was afraid to take that. He lingered over the body for a while, wondering if he should pull off and carry away some of the cloth that covered it, but then decided against it. The cloth would be useless to him as long as the summer lasted. He rolled the body into the brush and crept away.

The other two were sitting up beyond the fire. *His* woman was putting the cloth covering on her body; she had been naked as he crept back into his hiding place but now she was covering herself and pulling a bone thing through her hair. The knot on the top of her head had fallen away and now the light-colored hair hung down to her waist, almost touching the ground where she sat. The fighting woman sitting beside her picked up the knife belt and fastened it about the waist. They talked and laughed for a little while and then the fighter called through the timber to the dead one.

The dead one didn't answer.

The two climbed to their feet and approached the fire, still without alarm. The fighter reached down to pick up one of the black bricks. She touched her lips to the other woman's lips in some puzzling signal and then walked away from the fire to search for the missing one. The stalking man waited until she was gone from sight and slipped from his hiding place, crawling back to the edge where the body was concealed. He crouched in the grass at the shadow line, testing the wind and listening hard for his enemy. Near at hand he could smell the blood and urine of his victim, but he knew the enemy would miss it—the enemy were surprisingly blind and weak in warring skills.

The woman circled the stand of timber, calling out for the missing one. Her tone was conciliatory.

The stalking man tested her; he let her approach and walk by him, let her walk almost on him and the body nearby just to learn if she had the wit to see the mashed grasses and the nose to smell death. The woman did not. Her senses were inferior to his own and he felt a contempt for her. When she was by, when she was only a step past him, he sprang from the brush and sank the stolen knife into her back. It went in high and deep between the shoulder blades and he had to marvel again at the sharpness of it. The woman didn't even cry out or attempt a turn.

The stalker cut away her belt as before, but instead of hurling it into the darkness he thought to save the pouch which held her knife. He wasn't able to free it from the belt, nor was he able to fasten the belt about his own waist after cutting it, so in the end he cut off and threw away the stringed ears but kept the rest. The brick thing the woman had carried was another puzzle. It lacked the heft and familiarity of a good throwing stone, there was a hole in one side of it, and the object had a faint peculiar smell that was new to him. He tossed it into the brush after the two bodies. The scavengers could have it.

Making no attempt at concealment because the third woman was without weapons, he went through the trees toward the fire. *His* woman was there—he could smell the heady scent of her there.

She saw him coming and screamed.

The stalking man thought she would jump and run—he supposed she would flee blindly through the trees until she was in the open land beyond, and then run through that until she was lost and winded. He would pin her down then. Her naked body had been a delightful sight in the firelight and he wanted to put his fingers in the hair that hung to her waist.

The woman surprised him by staying down. She

scrabbled on her hands and knees toward the fire and grabbed up the black brick thing that had been left behind. He wasn't alarmed. He didn't think she had the strength to throw a hard stone and he suspected her aim was so poor he could easily dodge the missile.

She surprised him again by not lifting and hurling the black stone. She was on her knees on the other side of the fire and she seemed to be pushing the stone toward him, pushing it through the heated dust and ashes to him. She had not screamed after that first time.

THIRTEEN

Ice

The polar bear playfully seized him by the shoulder and shook him as easily as it would shake a fish scooped out of the icy water. It also spoke to him, despite having its mouth full.

"Wake up, Fisherman! The water's coming down. Come on, come on—*wake up!*"

Highsmith squirmed in the bed and opened one eye to stare up at the dim figure of the bear looming over him. It didn't resemble a bear now that he could see it more clearly, but it did have a painful clutch on his shoulder and it continued to shake him. The dormitory was dark. He sensed sleeping men around him.

"Go away!" Highsmith ordered.

"Water's coming down. The sergeant said to get you up. The sergeant said to bring you on the double."

Fisher Highsmith opened both eyes and looked up at the corporal. "What for? It must be midnight."

"It's almost morning—almost sunrise—and we got trouble. Now haul your ass out of that bed!"

Sleepily: "What's happening out there?"

"The rescue party's coming back, *everybody's* coming back from Regina. Bringing the wolves with them."

Highsmith sat upright. "My canoe!" He threw back the covers and reached for his clothing. The dormitory was chilly and he'd forgotten to hang his boots off the floor. They were frigid when he pushed his feet into them. In a moment he noticed an unusual quiet to the room and raised his head to listen. A silence. The two tiny windows weren't rattling, a surprising thing. "What happened to the storm?"

"It died off during the night."

"Good. That's good. Maybe we'll have a sunrise, and old-fashioned sunrise."

"I doubt it. We got a heavy cloud cover."

"Is the team bringing in my canoe?"

"I don't know, Fisherman, I don't care. I said they got *trouble*. Water's falling down on them."

"Water?"

"That's what I said. A stream of water, a whole river of water falling right there in the street, falling on their heads. The sergeant said on the double, Fisherman."

"Lake Agassiz! The lake is coming in on us!" Highsmith pushed the corporal into the aisle between the bed rows and set off at a trot. He noted that Jeanmarie and the doctor were gone from their beds. "Where is it falling? Were the men hurt? What are they bringing wolves for?"

The corporal hurried after him. "Which one first?"

"Where is it falling?"

"Right there in the street, in Regina, coming down out of the sky on their heads. They're mad, you bet!"

"Was anyone hurt?"

"Not from the water. They're wet, they liked'a drowned, I guess, but two of them got nipped by wolves."

"Why are they bringing the wolves back?"

"Fisherman, the damned wolves are *chasing* them. The rescue party got the other team out of the post office all safe and sound and everybody started home, but *then* the wolves took after them. When the men stopped to fight, the water came down on 'em. Damned near drowned everything—the men, the wolves, the sleds, everything!"

"I wish you had *called* me." Highsmith slammed through the dormitory door into the corridor.

"I just did," the corporal retorted.

The door to the hospital room was open but Highsmith never bothered to look in as he dashed past. His attention was concentrated on the spiral stairs and the communications tower at the top, and he turned a corner of the corridor so blindly he nearly ran down Jeanmarie coming the other way. She stepped nimbly aside.

"A stream of falling water!" he shouted.

Jeanmarie said: "Wellesley, Ontario, July 1880."

Highsmith didn't slow his pace.

When he burst into the tower room hurting for breath he found the security sergeant hunched over a transmitting unit listening to the sounds of a distant battle. The man's nose was only millimeters away from a small screen that displayed the letters "NP," but he watched those letters as intently as he would a picture. A small speaker below the screen emitted the ragged, blurping sound of gunfire while a peculiar sound in the background could only be the yelping and snarling of wolves.

"Do they have my canoe?" Highsmith asked eagerly.

The sergeant didn't turn. "Shuddup!"

A new voice said quickly: "We're moving, Sergeant. There's a half-dozen dead ones, maybe six or eight dead ones, and the rest of the pack has stopped to eat. We're moving."

"Good! Keep moving, get a lot of distance."

"Don't worry, we . . . " The radio voice hesitated, then said: "Oh, Sergeant, you won't believe this . . . !"

"The Fisherman is here with me," the security officer retorted. "I'll believe anything. What?"

"Somebody . . . somebody is firing at *us*."

"Somebody is doing what?"

"Somebody is firing stones and fish at us!" the voice declared. "Live fish! They're falling all over us, *on* us."

"I don't believe it," the sergeant said.

"Lake Agassiz!" Fisher Highsmith cried, running across the room to the transmitter. "No one is firing at you! You're on the bottom of the lake—water and fish and stones are falling down on you from the lake." He gripped the sergeant's shoulder. "Move them out of there before the whole lake falls on them!"

After a noticable hesitation the radio voice said: "I guess that was the Fisherman."

"It was, but keep the men moving. Put distance between you and those wolves." The sergeant paused in thought. He twisted his head to stare at Highsmith and then turned back to the transmitter. "Real live fish? Flopping fish?"

"Flopping all over the street. The water that came down first is turning to slush; it will freeze pretty soon. The fish are just flopping there in the slush. Shall I bring one to prove it?"

"Yes!" Highsmith shouted. "Washington South will be delighted with this. It proves my theory!"

"Keep moving, keep moving," the sergeant ordered.

When there was no reply from the speaker for long minutes, Highsmith pulled a chair from the nearest workbench and sat down behind the security officer. His nose caught an enticing aroma and he glanced around at the hot teapot. Immediately behind it was the same small area of melted ice on the window, where the constant heat kept open a visual passageway to the outside world. The same heaped snow was still visible through the passageway. When neither of the men in the room noticed his stare, Highsmith abruptly got up from the chair and helped himself at the teapot. He settled back with a hot cup, again with the impression of sitting in an igloo—an igloo with many of the comforts of modern civilization, of course. The tea was full-flavored.

It was gratifying to have his theories confirmed by independent observers. Charles Fort had never been so lucky. There were really two battles going on out there, *up* there. On the one level men of the present day were fighting wolves in their struggle to return to base, and on another level somewhere above them—a few thousand years from now—the mud-brick warriors were battling the invaders of their homeland. Some kind of melee was taking place on the waters of the lake, or on the shores, and the debris from that skirmish was falling on *this* level—much to the astonishment of the participants of this one. Fisher Highsmith saw himself in a remarkable position, a most unusual and historic position: he was the only man in the world who knew what was going on in both places. He sipped at the hot tea and admitted to himself it was a rightful honor.

The radio speaker suddenly broadcast a shrill scream, a piercing cry that seemed to begin in the middle of the cry itself and then climb to a high-pitched ending. A yelping of wolves surrounded the scream, and at once the blurping sound of gunfire began again.

Highsmith was on his feet. "They've got a woman up there!"

"There *ain't* no females on them teams, Fisherman," said the corporal. He was beside Highsmith, bending over the sergeant's chair to watch the "NP" on the screen.

"I heard a woman scream," Highsmith insisted.

"Please shuddup," the security officer commanded. He hunched over the microphone and speaker but kept his gaze on the small screen, as much a creature of habit as his second in command. Confused sounds of struggle blared from the speaker. Someone was shouting directions over the cries of his own men and the yelping of the wolves, over the drumming gunfire that had quickly intensified. It was difficult to guess whether the men or the animals had been the more surprised by the unexpected development. The scream did not come again.

"There just *ain't* no females!"

Highsmith looked at him and said quietly: "Eighteen."

The sergeant craned his neck to look up at them. He held his tongue but stared dubiously at the recon man.

Highsmith pointed a bony finger at the transmitter. "Eighteen is down. I *said* she was due. Tell the men to put her in a thermal sack, and quickly—before she freezes. Ask them if she needs medical attention. I'll alert Harley. The men must bring her in at once."

The sergeant continued to stare at him. "The old bourbon again, Fisherman?" He was disapproving.

"Certainly not! Not before breakfast. I tell you, Eighteen *is* down. The men must put her in a sack at once."

The radio speaker erupted behind the sergeant's back. "Sergeant—? Sergeant—?" Tangled sounds of battle underwrote the urgency in the distant man's voice.

"I'm here." The security officer remembered himself and turned back to his microphone. "I'm here."

"Now, Sergeant, you won't believe *this* . . ."

"Yes, I will." There was an odd note in the man's voice, a note that suggested he was tired, or cross, or perhaps had suffered from interrupted sleep. "I believe you. You've picked up a woman. She fell down out of the sky on your heads. She fell down with the water and the flopping fish and the stones, and she fell on somebody coming down. I believe you, mister." As an afterthought, he added: "Her number is Eighteen."

The radio hesitation was pronounced but the far voice finally said: "We've picked up a woman. She fell down out of the sky, but she fell on those wolves coming down. She smashed up a couple of them—killed them dead. There is a lot of confusion around here, Sergeant."

"No more than here," the sergeant retorted. "Get the woman in a thermal sack before she freezes. I don't guess she's dressed for this weather."

"That's the funny part . . ." the voice said.

The security officer looked at Highsmith again but didn't trust himself to reply.

Highsmith asked: "Funny in what way?"

"She's naked," the distant man said. "Naked to the waist and all chewed up. I think she tangled with a bear."

Highsmith nodded wisely. "Eighteen."

Forty men and four sleds were crowding into the shop from the wintry dawn outside, men attached to each other by lifelines and some of them bunched so closely together their outstretched hands were riding the shoulders of the men next in front. They resembled snowmen, ice men moving through the doors pulling sleds behind them. The sled runners grated on cold concrete. Through the open doors a thin yellowish line limned the eastern horizon, telling the coming sunrise behind a cloud cover. The world outside was frozen and its breath chilled the shop.

Highsmith fastened his gaze on the first sled, the sled containing a body in a thermal sack. The sack was connected to a heater; it was securely lashed with rope and someone had loaded a fragment of a dugout canoe atop it where the feet of the passenger should be. Highsmith looked at the canoe fragment with small interest.

Harley knelt beside the sled and tugged at the ropes securing its burden. His prying fingers were not equal to the task, and somebody brushed past him to do the job with a knife. A man at the other end of the sled picked up the piece of canoe and thrust it into Highsmith's hands.

"Now shut up about this damned thing," the man said. He peered at the reconstructionist through cold eyes. "You *are* Highsmith, aren't you?"

"Yes. But where did you—?"

"Pleased to meet you, maybe. My name is Massenet. I was tempted to throw that chunk of wood overboard."

"Where did you find it?"

"I didn't find it. The other team did."

"No, no, I don't mean that. The canoe fragment was found somewhere on the north side of the city. Where did you find this woman?"

"In the street, on the southwest side. We picked her up on the way home"

"How far apart? Can you make an estimate how far apart they were found—the canoe and the woman?"

"I don't know the place where they picked up the canoe," Massenet answered. "But if it was on the north side—oh, three kilometers, maybe four. A considerable distance."

Highsmith's gaze went back to the thermal sack. "*She* couldn't have been paddling the canoe."

"Nobody paddles canoes in this weather. She was busy fighting bears, or big cats."

"Will she live?"

"Ask the doctor."

Harley was picking at the sack, struggling to open the noosed neck of it. Only a hole the size of a thumb had been left open for air. The tie lines had been removed and the sacked body lay free on the sled. The man who had cut the ropes reached down again and cut the knot at the top.

Highsmith felt an uneasy movement in his stomach but bent down beside the sled to help the doctor. Together they pulled at the frozen cords and got the sack open. A wealth of long black hair was exposed, and then the woman's face. Highsmith stared with a new fascination.

"Give me that knife," Harley demanded. "Give it to me! We can cut this sack away and—God in Heaven!"

Fisher Highsmith was on his feet and running for the back doors. Someone was sliding them shut as he approached, but he grabbed a door with one hand and hurled himself through it into the frigid false dawn outside. His stomach erupted and he doubled over with the agony of it, gasping for breath as he fought to control the spasmodic vomiting. He was not aware of the intense cold. The sickening image of a woman mauled first by a bear, or a cat, and then by wolves tortured his mind and stomach.

Daylight was at the window, day without sunshine. The ready room was a refuge of quiet normality. The pilot was gone from his cot and the absence of sounds was a pronounced relief after the many days and weeks of snoring. The pilot was outside, watching the crew repair his aircraft. Jeanmarie was sitting next to Highsmith at her own bench, but she wasn't reading or working on the maps; she was doing nothing. The polylibrarian sat quietly in her chair with her hands folded in her lap, only looking at the reconstructionist and waiting for him to speak—if he cared to speak at all. Harley was still missing from the tableau. The room's one really bright light illuminated an empty place on the rug where the doctor liked to sit and knit when he wasn't busy elsewhere. There was nothing but distant kitchen sounds where the personnel were eating breakfast.

Fisher Highsmith huddled in his chair wrapped in a blanket and wished the ache would go away. He hadn't done *that* in years and he'd forgotten the miserable sensation of it, forgotten the lingering aftereffects. He gently rubbed his sore stomach and wondered if he dared sample the bourbon now. The stoneware jug rested on the bench before him but caution stopped his hand; bourbon might not sit too well on an upset stomach.

He said in a low voice: "They are coming in like stragglers from a lost battle, survivors from an unknown disaster. But we know the battle now, and we know the antagonists. I wish we could fix the time."

"You may succeed in that."

"Maybe. Did you see her?"

"Yes. I was struck by the skin coloring."

"A southerner? A tropical person?"

"It is quite possible."

"She had long black hair down around her shoulders. Pretty. I wonder what color her eyes are?"

"I would expect brown."

"A tropical person," he mused aloud. "Are the invaders coming in from Central or South America? From Yucatan, or Panama, or Brazil? Do they speak Spanish? Portuguese?"

Jeanmarie said: "The tropical and subtropical zones would be the most favorable to life during a glacial advance. Eiseley has said that man lived in the tropics during the last glaciation, and that he moved out to follow the retreating ice sheets northward."

"Carrying fire. But didn't *some* men stay in the north during the ice? Didn't stragglers stay behind?"

"They did in Europe, and future discovery may establish their presence in North America as well. Discoveries in France and Spain have revealed that a type of primitive man continued to live there despite the presence of ice only a few hundred kilometers away. As far as is known, glaciation has not covered a whole continent. You will remember that the last ice did not advance much beyond a line drawn between St. Louis and Cincinnati."

Highsmith thought of his artifacts: the mud bricks, a broken bow, a polygon, the superior knives. "Perhaps *she* came up from South America, but when she got here she found old Seventeen standing in the way. She gunned him aside."

The thermal sack had been emptied of its burden in the small hospital room rather than the shop. Harley insisted on decorum. Eighteen had been placed in the bed across the room from Seventeen but nobody remarked the juxtaposition. It hadn't been necessary this time to chase base personnel from the room. When the male nurse closed the door only his wife, the doctor, and himself were closed in with the two recoveries. After a while the male nurse brought out the new patient's clothing and gave them to Highsmith.

"Doctor said the battle goes on. He said you would understand that."

Fisher Highsmith stared at the clothing now spread out over his workbench.

The topmost object was a medallion affixed to a bright metal chain, an object to be worn about the neck; it appeared to be bronze and had small figures etched into the surface. Jeanmarie had reached for the medallion and held it close for inspection, revealing to Highsmith that something more was printed or cut into the backside of the artifact.

The single tailored garment could only be a pair of close-fitting trousers, despite its present state of sad disrepair. The pattern was cut snug at the waist and over the thighs, and then followed slim legs down to a point near the ankle where they ended with straps meant to be fastened under the arch of the foot. The cloth was a pale blue with thin gold piping running full length down the outside seam of each leg, suggesting a dress uniform rather than a field garment intended for rough duty. The trousers had been cut or torn in many places, indicating the owner's struggle with animals, and cut again where the doctor had stripped them away a short while ago. At the bottom of one leg near the strap the gold piping had been ripped away to reveal the threads beneath. Highsmith picked absently at the threads and studied the pale-blue uniform. He noted its small size and glanced at Jeanmarie's trousered legs.

The only remaining objects on the bench were the boots. One of them had been chewed away at the heel, reminding him of his queasy stomach, but the other was a whole boot of excellent workmanship; it was a short boot of soft leather resembling suede, with a hard sole and a broad heel showing wear. It was in keeping with the uniform, and the uniform fitted the wearer.

He inspected the medallion. "A good luck charm?"

"Military insignia."

Highsmith turned it over. The obverse side pictured crossed knives beneath a simple crown—knives closely akin to the blade that had come down with Seventeen. Highsmith studied them for a moment and turned the medallion back over.

"What is this? Do you recognize this?"

"It may represent the number eight."

He said: "It doesn't look like—" but stopped.

"The figure resembles the old Hebrew *cheth* and the Greek *eta,* both of which were symbols for the numeral eight."

Highsmith turned the piece around trying to read a number into it. "Do you think this is Hebrew or Greek?"

"No, but it may be a derivative of either one."

"The Eighth Army? The Eighth Corps?"

"Perhaps the garrison of the eighth city, or the care-taker troops of the eighth zone."

"What's this other side, the crown and swords?"

She said: "The obverse is a common symbol denoting loyalty to and protection for a sovereign. It has many counterparts throughout history."

"Our soldier fought for a king?"

"I would suspect a queen."

He eyed the woman beside him. "I *said* you were the enemy, Jeanmarie. All of Seventeen's enemies are female. Some matriarchy, somewhere, is hell-bent on conquest."

She nodded somberly but said nothing.

"But I don't understand why she was found three or four kilometers away from the canoe; the battle should have been fought at the place where the canoe was found. But this *does* prove something else, Jeanmarie. It proves that at least one of the blue-eyed warriors has a polygon and knows how to use it. I've been waiting for something like this."

"Washington South will have to be impressed."

"They will *now*. The bureaucrats can't very well ignore the evidence now; not with those two in sick bay, and the polygon, and all this." He waved a hand over the uniform. "This will complete my report, this and the artifacts and the maps and your history book. This about closes the case." He glanced with pride at his map of the future.

Breakfast was only half successful.

Fisher Highsmith had thought that something warm and soft and non-controversial would not only ease the pangs in his stomach but smooth the way for a better day ahead. He asked the cook for two soft-poached eggs on lightly toasted brown bread. Cook's helper laughed hilariously, pretending to find genuine humor in the request, but the cook only stared at Highsmith with an expression best not translated.

Highsmith picked up a bowl of lumpy oatmeal and found a seat across from the doctor.

"This stuff tastes like sawdust!"

Harley peered at the bowl through bifocals. "It may be."

"Do we *have* to have sawdust in the oatmeal?"

"If you want to go on eating, you do. When was the last time you saw wheat or oats growing north of Duluth?"

"I don't know," Highsmith admitted.

"I do. It was the year after I lost my horse." Harley pointed at the bowl. "Eat your sawdust. Your children will grow up on it. They *will,* or they'll grow hungry."

Highsmith and his stomach thought it best to change the subject. "How is our new patient?"

"She's in good physical condition, considering."

"Considering what?"

"Considering the punishment she took."

"Well, yes—she *did* get shot down by a primitive."

"No."

"No?" Why not?"

"That woman wasn't shot down. A lot of nasty things happened to her but she wasn't shot by your polygon. There isn't a trace of radiation burn on her body. There isn't."

"But, Harley, I saw the—" He stopped to reconsider what he had seen when the thermal sack was opened. "Harley, according to my theory these people can't drop down here on us unless they are fired on. They *can't* fall down on us from the future unless the polygon knocks them down."

"So concoct a new theory. Make a hole for them to fall through."

"A hole in what?"

"In anything: air, water, dirt. Do it."

"She had to be fired on, or at, or *something.* The gun must have been used." He waved a spoonful of oatmeal. "Maybe a primitive fired at her in the water. She's *here.*"

"Undeniably, she's here. Maybe she was taking a swim with her pants and boots on, maybe a passing canoe hit her, maybe she came down with those fish because she's a mermaid."

"Harley, what are you talking about?"

"I'm trying to say," Harley answered patiently, "that *before* the patient tumbled into the water she took a blow at the base of the skull that must have stunned her. Maybe that toppled her in. Somebody did strike her from behind. But before that she was clawed by a cat, some big animal that did its best to take the skin off. It damned near *did*." He shook an admonishing finger. "She was wearing those pants when the cat hit her. Go look at them, look at the rents. Claws, not knives, Fisherman. And finally she came down on the wolves. She has a monstrous bruise to show for *that*."

"Was there a shirt?"

"No shirt. It had been removed."

"Did a primitive try to rape her?"

"With her pants on?"

Highsmith stirred oatmeal. "A big cat? A tiger?"

"Not up here, not in the northern states. We have bears, foxes, wolves, lynxes, smaller animals with claws."

After a while Highsmith said: "I'll think of something. I'll find a way to fit her into my model. We scientific types pride ourselves on our imaginations."

"I'm sure you will," the doctor said. "We doctor types just patch up patients and autopsy the losers."

Highsmith's stomach wished the doctor hadn't said that. "I'll finish my paper today or tomorrow," he promised. "You can read it before I send it down south."

"Make it a good story. Send me a copy—I'll read it."

"But you can read it first, as soon as I finish it."

Harley shook his head. "I'm leaving."

Highsmith was thunderstruck. "When?"

"Ask Jeanmarie. As soon as the hospital craft is ready to fly. We've been ordered to Billings."

"Who is *we?*"

"The patients, the nurses, Jeanmarie, me. The agency has issued orders to leave as soon as possible, to take advantage of the weather. The agency is anxious to transfer those two recoveries to Billings Hospital—they want to *see* live bodies. This base is shutting down, Fisherman. Now eat your oatmeal."

"But you can't leave just like that! The base isn't supposed to close for weeks yet. Not for several days, anyway. Why are you taking Jeanmarie?"

"Ask Jeanmarie," the doctor replied. "She accepted the transfer orders."

Fisher Yann Highsmith dropped his spoon into the sawdusted oatmeal and pushed back from the table. "Excuse me." He left the commissary with undue haste, nearly running down the two nurses coming through the door for their breakfasts. "Excuse me," he said again, and dodged around them to hurry along the corridor. His imagination said that he heard voices as he sped past the closed hospital door.

The ready room was empty. The pilot was still outside overseeing the repair of his aircraft. Jeanmarie's chair at her bench was as vacant as his own. The pictophone was dark. His leaping imagination told him that he *had* heard voices behind the closed door. Highsmith snatched up the bronze medallion from the bench and darted into the corridor.

A voice was clearly audible in the hospital room.

He knocked quickly and pushed in. "Jeanmarie—" Highsmith stopped in the doorway with astonishment.

Jeanmarie was perched on the patient's bed, perched on the edge of the bed and holding Eighteen's hand in the manner a fond relative or a visiting spouse would hold hands with an ailing family member. They were in close and sympathetic contact. His gaze moved from the warm handclasp to Jeanmarie's face, and he found annoyance there. Her expression said he was an interloper. He let his gaze drift on to the queen's warrior and met open hostility. The woman's eyes were brown, and unfriendly.

Highsmith said: "I . . . Harley said . . ."

Jeanmarie asked: "Please sit down." She indicated the only chair in the room, a folding chair placed in the far corner at the foot of Seventeen's bed. "I have established communication. Please do not interrupt."

"She's talking to you!" Highsmith exclaimed.

"*Please,* sit down," she said again. There was an edge to her voice in keeping with the expression on her face.

Fisher Highsmith retreated and sat down. Jeanmarie had never spoken to him like that in all the two or three weeks he'd known her. He stared at the two women with undisguised curiosity, while the unfriendly brown eyes stared back.

Eighteen asked a sudden question, a question not readily understood because the words tended to run together. They suggested a once-recognizable tongue now altered and debased by time. Three or four or five thousand years of time. Highsmith needed to repeat the question in his mind before getting the true sense of it, before deciphering it. His Spanish wasn't all that good to begin with and the degeneration only made matters worse

"*T'amig?*" Her voice was hoarse.

Jeanmarie hesitated only long enough to be certain of the intent. "*No tengo ningun amigo.*" She spoke slowly and clearly to enable the newcomer to translate what would be incredibly ancient and stilted Spanish.

Highsmith didn't think that answer quite fair, after puzzling out the sense of the question. He *was* Jeanmarie's friend and she should have admitted it. At the same time, he realized that Jeanmarie wasn't aware he understood the question and the answer, however feeble his grasp of Spanish. As a polylibrarian her knowledge of that and a number of other languages was taken for granted, but he was mildly disappointed that she failed to credit him this one tongue. And now she denied having a friend—especially him.

"*T'bajo'd'sclavo?*"

Jeanmarie made answer before Highsmith could separate the words. He had about decided that the intent of the question was "Is he your slave?" or "Is he slave labor?" when the polylibrarian answered in careful fashion.

"*No. El Yanqui.*" As if that explained everything. But it didn't; the patient revealed puzzlement.

Jeanmarie said: *"Obrero y escritor."*

Highsmith thought he could agree with that. He *was* a workman in the sense of being a skilled reconstructionist, an artisian, and he *was* a writer although that skill was but secondary to his profession. The written report he would send to Washington South would be a masterpiece of deduction and reconstruction, a model paper, and even now Eighteen was adding to that report.

The hostile brown eyes studied him a moment longer and looked away, dismissing him. Highsmith guessed that he wouldn't amount to much in her native land, in Yucatan or Brazil or wherever. Not in a matriarchy.

He held up the bronze medallion. "Ask about this."

Eighteen put a quick hand to her throat and found the insignia missing. She made as if to rise from the bed but Jeanmarie calmed her, pressed her down again.

Jeanmarie said: "Please bring it here, carefully."

Highsmith handed over the artifact and retreated to his chair. He watched Jeanmarie as she placed the chain about the patient's neck and fastened it. They both seemed pleased that the medallion was in its rightful place.

"El ejercito Octavo?"

Eighteen answered: *"Bat'lon 'tavo."*

Highsmith made a mental note: she was a part of the Eighth Battalion, of her queen's occupation army. He kept a straight face as Jeanmarie made translation for him.

"Find out her country," he urged the polylibrarian. "Find out where she came from."

"I have already done so," Jeanmarie replied impatiently. "Her place of origin appears to be southern Mexico."

"Mexico!" Highsmith exclaimed. *"That's* the place to be, *that's* the safe refuge until after the ice. Harley's wife is down there. I'm going down there." Highsmith paused to consider his own words and was struck by what he'd said. "Jeanmarie, these enemy warriors will be our own children! I mean, this is our own posterity coming back to conquer the States—to occupy North

America. Our own descendents!" He stared at the woman in the bed with a new fascination.

"It would appear so."

"It *is* so." He eyed Eighteen with some distrust. "I don't think I want to be *her* grandfather." And he looked again at their clasped hands and interlaced fingers. "Ask her how far down the ice went, ask her the southernmost limits of glaciation. Did it go beyond St. Louis this time?"

Jeanmarie began framing the question.

They were distracted by a ripping sound and the bed moved under Highsmith's hand. He jerked around in his chair to find Seventeen struggling to sit up. The oxygen tent was torn away as the battered warrior came upright. Seventeen pulled at the restraining strap fastening his arm to the bed, but could not free it. The bottle of IV hanging above him swayed and threatened to fall from its hanger. The tube feeding the liquid down from the IV bottle into a needle inserted in a vein at the back of his hand worked loose, and seemed ready to fall free. Seventeen growled at the puzzling entanglements and again jerked at them, seeking freedom. His attention was caught by a movement at the foot of the bed and he turned to meet Highsmith's alarmed gaze.

Fisher Highsmith said: "Good morning, Defender."

Seventeen roared his answer, his disdain of Highsmith and his anger at the world. He pulled at the strap holding him to the bed. The needle was torn from his hand and the tube dripped liquid over the bed and the floor. The bottle of IV would soon follow. The bed rocked and jounced as the man sought to tear himself loose. His rage was mounting.

Jeanmarie cried: "Get the doctor! Quickly!"

Highsmith jumped from his chair, and knew the mistake.

Seventeen swung at the sound of the voice. He found Jeanmarie and in the following moment found another woman in the opposite bed. That other woman was trying to sit up but was also restricted by bottle, tube, and injection needle. The thundering roar had to be heard all through the building.

"Kilm!"

Fisher Highsmith stepped between the beds and learned his second mistake.

Seventeen swung his feet to the floor and threw his battered body past Highsmith, seeking his enemies. The restraining strap held fast, and the bed toppled over on Fisher with the crushing force of a load of mud bricks. The IV bottle plummeted to the floor behind. Highsmith went down with the bed on top of him, crying his surprise and hurt. He hadn't known a bed could be so heavy.

Seventeen was down beside him but not as flat as he was. The unkempt warrior kept going, crawling across the room on one hand and his knees and dragging the bed with him. That man was intent only on reaching the two women.

"Kilm!"

Highsmith grabbed at the warrior's foot, hoping to stop the maniac, but got that foot in his face as reward. He felt his nose bleeding and a stinging pain rocking his head. The bed was dragged across his prone body until the worn restraining strap finally parted and freed the warrior.

Highsmith cried: "Watch out! He's loose!"

He was dumfounded at what happened next. He watched Eighteen tear herself loose from the IV apparatus and leap from her bed. For a hectic moment only her bare feet were within his line of sight, running toward him, and then they vanished momentarily as she sprang into the air and came down hard on her enemy's unprotected back. Seventeen crashed down, howling his new pain as the stump of his severed arm struck the floor. He twisted away and tried to climb to his knees. The fighting woman struck him with something, smashed a cruel blow to his head, and he fell again in numbing agony. The woman swiftly knelt beside him and grounded a gun.

Highsmith cried out: "No—don't do that! *No!*"

Eighteen had the hospital's cardiogun at her enemy's head, trying to ram a hole through that head. Highsmith saw the expression on the woman's face and felt a quick relief. The cardiogun would not fire by a simple grounding, despite the angry and frustrated efforts of its operator. There was no discharge. Eighteen slammed the butt to the floor, then rammed it again against the laboring warrior's skull. The hated enemy didn't vanish in a half-seen blur of purplish light, and the woman screamed her bitter disappointment at the failure. Highsmith thought it sounded more like a blasphemous curse.

From a distance, from a thousand kilometers away although it was just across the room, he heard Jeanmarie's answering cry.

"Gatillo! Aprieta el gatillo!"

"Don't say that! Jeanmarie, don't—"

Eighteen found the trigger of the cardiogun and held it down. The muzzle was pressed against her antagonist's skull. Seventeen died under the electromagnetic impulses of an instrument designed to shock and manipulate a faltering heart. His limbs jerked and shuddered in response to the brain convulsions, and he died in agony.

Fisher Highsmith didn't hear the door being slammed open, but he did see Harley's foot come down on the woman's wrist, freeing the gun from her fingers.

FOURTEEN

Iron

The scribe caught sight of his first barbarian when the supply boat put in to shore for meat and fresh water. The native was as fiercely ugly as legend said him to be.

The sighting brought a crowd to the deck.

The supply boat had been following the western shore of the river since lifting anchor at sunrise, and now it stood at least eight hours upriver. The sun was just past the zenith and already the summer heat was withering. The scribe admitted to himself he'd been wrong about that. He hadn't wanted to leave home and sail north; people *said* it was bitterly cold on the frontier, people *said* the great ice sheets would freeze one overnight, people *said* there was no warmth anywhere after three or four days from port, but people—and he among them —had been wrong about that. The summer sun of the frontier proved them all wrong and he sought the shade whenever he was on deck. Sticky, sweltering heat smothered the river and the prairies on either side. Sweat was under his shirt.

Of course, there was ice *somewhere* in the northland. Massive walls of ice stretched across the rim of civilization from Elena's Greatwest Mountains to Elena's Northeast Sea, literally blocking the frontier, but that ice was yet many weeks away at their present rate of travel. The supply boat was tediously slow. He would see the ice scarp in due time, and would learn for himself the truth or falsity of those fantastic stories brought back by troops once stationed near the walls. He was confident he wouldn't freeze if he stayed back a prudent distance. It was a bit ridiculous even to think of freezing under the same sun that smothered the river.

The scribe joined the curious crowd on the foredeck and stared in open-mouthed wonder at the barbarian— who stared at them in like fashion. It was likely the savage had never seen a boat before.

The scribe carried an open notebook in his hand but he made no effort to write or sketch. The note book served as his badge of office, his ticket of admission to those higher circles and private places that otherwise would be closed to him. Elena the Brat had awarded him a commission. Elena had given him a supply of notebook and a letter of introduction and sent him forth to observe, listen, sketch, and record; sent him forth to write the living history of the frontier even while the campaign to conquer it was under way. To be accurate, Elena's ministers had sent him forth to observe, listen, sketch, and record; but it was all done in her name, of course. For the present, in her name the ministers were operating the government to suit themselves.

The barbarian was poised for flight.

He was a burly brute, a shaggy and unkempt fellow who wore some kind of baggy pouch or animal skin about his loins to cover his private parts. Some of the troops pressed against the gunwales made ribald comment on that. The barbarian was incredibly dirty; his matted hair hung down over his head and face to merge and grow together with an equally filthy beard, and if the boat happened to be downwind of the fellow his smell would be equally foul. He carried a bow and a crude knife of sorts, with a packet of arrows slung across one shoulder. His feet were bare and blackened with dirt, and in all he was an unprepossessing welcome to the new world of the frontier.

The scribe guessed that the barbarian had been stalking wild cattle when he was discovered, the same wild cattle the ship's company was intent on capturing and butchering when they put to shore. The savage had appeared suddenly out of the prairie grass, losing his cover when he stood up to stare at the approaching boat.

Two sailors jumped over the side and waded ashore with a tieline. Someone on deck forgot herself and shouted an order, and the barbarian took flight with a speed that was truly astonishing. The scribe hadn't believed that anyone could run so fast. He put a hand to his eyes to shade the sun and followed the running man until he was no more than a stick figure blending and losing himself against a distant stand of timber. Unfortunately the cattle took fright as well, and the ship's company would have to be content with fresh water and a romp in the prairie grass.

The scribe followed his troops over the side to stretch his legs.

The queen-to-be: people called her Elena the Chaste, perhaps because she was only nine years old.

The scribe called her the Brat because he knew the future queen somewhat better than her subjects thought they did. He'd known the child since her birth but he took care not to call her "brat" aloud because of a healthy aversion to jails—although he had reason to believe that some of her ministers shared his silent disrespect. One could only hope that Elena the Brat was transformed into a mature and reasonable adult before she became a queen seven years hence. Her mother wouldn't have permitted the child's spoilage, had the good lady lived. Her mother had been a warm and decent individual, beyond having a greedy lust for more and ever more territory to rule. The crown already possessed every *milla* of land, mountain, and lake between the great river canyon splitting the Zona Desert in the north and that smaller and soggy ravine to the south that separated the continents. But Elena's mother hadn't been content.

Her lust for empire eventually led him north.

The scribe hadn't wanted to give up his comfortable home and haunts to travel north; he had not the slightest wish to visit the new frontier opened by the Brat's mother, to feel the icy breath of its frozen walls, to risk his skin among the bloody barbarians. The idea was appalling. He was content with his lot, and even the suggestion that he abandon his untroubled life to live and travel with the troops was shocking. Yet here he was. He suspected that one of the Brat's ministers was responsible for his present position, that some one of those ministers had been annoyed or angered by one of his guidebooks, or by his commentaries on court life, and had arranged his commission in Elena's name when the time was ripe.

He had first come to the court's attention by publishing a visitor's guidebook to Mecali, the royal city, recounting the visual delights of that metropolis, the magnificent gardens, the stately buildings, the wide avenues with no sewage running in the streets, the ordered house of government. He led the tourist through the museum, the better eating establishments, the archeological ruins, and the pleasure places where the wealthy and the army officers spent their spare time. That last earned him his first audience with the Brat's mother. The lady read those passages aloud in his presence and asked him if he were indulging in poetic license. He'd assured her that he was not, that the places of pleasure *did* cater to the wealthy civilians and the officers of her army. She seemed bemused by that. She had him describe the houses in some detail and describe various activities that took place there. None of it appeared to shock her, although it was evident she was hearing some matters for the first time. She commented on her officers' taste.

The scribe had entered the audience expecting her wrath, and jail, but instead that meeting was the beginning of a friendship that lasted the few remaining years of her life. He became the only scribe favored by the court, and soon began writing commentaries on royal life. He got along well with most of the ministers, and prospered. When Elena was born, it was he who suggested the child's name by pointing to an ancester of the same name who had played a romantic role in history. The Brat had never thanked him. For that matter, the Brat didn't seem to care whether he lived or died. Her swollen ego was wholly filled by her self.

Elena the Brat was nine years old, and the frontier had been expanded to the point where troops were now stationed permanently within sight of the retreating ice. Mopping-up operations had been under way for a number of years but were not yet complete: the barbarians were a stubborn lot who clung to the land and fought back in treacherous ways. Someone, some minister or general with idiotic dreams of glory, had decided to increase the intensity of the campaign and secure the safety of the new land before the end of seven years. In just seven more years Elena would be of age and would be crowned queen. The anonymous someone had the inspired notion that a wholly conquered and well-secured colony would be a splendid gift, an unparalleled gift to present the newly crowned queen on her birthday. A brand-new world ready for her exploitation. To that end, large numbers of troops and a never-ending line of supply boats were directed north to accomplish the task in the allotted time. Victory was inevitable.

Just as inevitably, another someone—perhaps an annoyed or maligned minister—had reasoned that a scribe should accompany the troops to observe, listen, sketch, and record the final campaign. That scribe would write the living history of the conquest and in seven years' time the finished work would be presented to the newly crowned Elena with the gift of the territory.

The Brat hadn't bothered to say goodbye when he sailed.

The supply boat was sixteen days upriver when it hove to within sight of the landing that was its destination, and dropped anchor. An absence of life about the landing aroused instant suspicions. The wharf itself was empty, not only of human life but of the military supplies that had been left there a few days earlier by the last boat in; the few buildings that housed the landing personnel were standing open and deserted. There was not even smoke in the chimneys from kitchen fires.

Someone pointed out the abandoned motorwagon standing in the dusty street. That hauler was not assigned to the landing; a number painted on the side indicated its service area, and its dead position in the street told its aborted mission. The hauler had come in from some distant outpost for supplies off the dock but was still facing the river landing, not backed up to it for loading. The searchlight atop the wagon had been smashed by rocks.

The scribe crouched behing the shield of the gunwale and felt his first real fright.

With the others he searched the landing area for some sign of life, for some sign of the defenders or the enemy, but like the others he found nothing. Even the bodies of the defenders were missing from the scene and he wondered what had been done with them; he was not so naïve as to believe that *all* the defenders, *all* the personnel who worked the dock had gone chasing off across country after a fleeing enemy. The troops might have done that, but the civilian dockworkers and their administrator would have stayed behind.

A smallboat was put over the side and four soldiers armed with quarterguns were rowed ashore. The scribe watched them go, knowing the reason for their deployment. The guns were useless on board and on the wharf, and the task force would approach the settlement from a flanking position ashore in order to protect the boat and its company when the craft put in and tied up. Those quarterguns were the real security.

When the smallboat returned, crews hoisted the anchor and maneuvered the supply boat toward the deserted landing. The scribe kept watch on the four soldiers working their careful way along the shore. He admired their professionalism and knew that if trouble came those four would find it first. Above him and around him where he crouched the dozen soldiers remaining on board waited with arms at ready; they carried unsheathed knives in the one hand and the inutile quarterguns in the other.

The supply boat crept in to the landing.

The scribe moved his gaze from the four on shore to the empty buildings just beyond the wharf. Their doors were hanging open. He had the quick suspicion that the enemy could be concealed inside, waiting on the landing party, but then he realized the troopers would suspect the same thing and be alert for that possibility. The buildings would be the first to be searched and erased if the enemy lurked there. His watch went back to the four on shore.

He saw them kneeling at the far end of the dusty street where the street ended and the prairie began. They had separated, taking positions to cover the settlement and those points of the compass to either side where attack might be expected. There was no other movement between them and the river. Two sailors slipped over the side of the boat and tied up to the landing. They hauled the boat alongside it, gunwale to dockside, and tied off astern.

The scribe's ears were stung by the shrill blast of an officer's whistle. The officer had been standing just behind, and now she gave him a sharp but friendly rap on the top of his head as she vaulted over him. The dozen troopers went over the side after her and raced along the wharf, all intent on the yawning doorways. The scribe shouted after them to hurry but it was an unnecessary warning. They ran for solid earth and a solid grounding for the quarterguns. An answering shout came from the far end of the street and he looked back to the four who waited there.

One of those soldiers was up and running, racing toward the motorwagon, toward the dock and the boat and *him*. The other three were scrambling aside, scrambling for favorable positions at either side of the street. They cried warning.

He saw the cause for the alarm.

The rear door of the big hauler was thrown open and the enemy tumbled out, uncounted numbers of them jumping to the dusty street and fanning out to meet the soldiers coming up from the river. Their noise and numbers were frightening. They came out in a roiling undisciplined mass, easy targets, but armed with every kind of primitive weapon the scribe had seen or heard described. They were a howling mob. The lone soldier racing toward the hauler dropped to her knees to ground the quartergun, then snatched it up again without fire. The scribe knew why: for a paralyzing moment he had looked into the muzzle of the weapon.

The kneeling woman had put herself in an impossible position: she could not fire at the hauler and the enemy without hitting her own companions coming up behind them, and without erasing the dock and the supply boat moored at the end of it. All were in her line of fire. She tried to get up, wanting a better position on either side of the street, but was knocked flat and breathless when a howling knot of men overran her. She managed to ground the quartergun and fire once, away from the mo-

torwagon, and then she and her savage adversaries flickered and were swept from the street—all of them erased
by someone else firing blindly from across the street.
That other woman lived only a little longer, only a
breath or two before the enemy found her.

The howling mob spilled down onto the wharf.

Some of the soldiers had managed to reach the earth-
en banks beyond the wharf but others had not. They
fought where they met the horde. Those few on solid
ground found themselves in almost the same positions
that had defeated the scout in the street: they could
ground and fire away from the boat and the dock, but
not toward it where the greater melee was taking place.
Those few on solid ground gave a good accounting while
they lived; they swept the dusty street before them and
the empty buildings lining the street, they erased the
motorwagon and some of the enemy still clustered
around it, they cleansed the area at the head of the dock
and then turned with blades to fight on the dock as savagely as their foe. An unprotected belly was always the
first target in close-quarter combat.

The wooden planking underfoot grew slippery with
residuum. The battle raged in the hot morning sunlight
at an hour or so before the zenith. The boat and its supplies were the prizes sought by the marauders.

The scribe caught sight of his last barbarian when the
man climbed over the gunwale with an ax in his hand.
The native was as fiercely ugly as legend said him to be.

FIFTEEN

Ice

The sun was shining brightly on the day the last load was flown out from base camp. It was the only day of brilliant sun and clear sky in several weeks, and Fisher Yann Highsmith thought it a mocking way to bid him farewell. The outside temperature was a negative forty degrees.

Bare rooms.

The reconstructionist stalked through the deserted base marveling at the differences presented by an empty room, by a succession of empty rooms. Walking into a newly emptied room was like walking up to a stranger who resembled an old acquaintance. The shops had been stripped of gear and that gear flown out to Duluth and to Sudbury in eastern Ontario. The sleds, the generators, and the heaters had been needed in Sudbury but the remainder of the equipment was put in storage in Duluth against the day that city, like Billings, would be abandoned and its inhabitants relocated. Only the fixtures remained. The lighting and the workbenches were written off and left behind, together with a few stubby brooms and a shovel with a broken handle. Empty oil cans were stacked along a wall. The cold floor revealed many parallel lines where sled runners had scraped over it, and a few pieces of rope scrap lay where they had fallen. The bench at which Highsmith had laboriously put together a polygon artifact and a mud-brick ravelin was littered with debris no one had bothered to sweep away. Snow seeped in under the doors.

The ravelin, carefully cut into sections, was crated and loaded aboard the aircraft for shipment to Washington South. Accompanying that crate were two smaller boxes. One contained the broken bow, the prized knife, and the polygon weapon that was still operative, together with its poorly reconstructed twin that was not; the weapons were packed away with a pair of boots, the tattered trousers, and a replica of a bronze medallion. The second and last box contained his map of the future together with a manuscript explaining it, and the copy of Charles Fort's old history book that Jeanmarie had given him. The whole of his work. All that would go to Washington South with him.

Highsmith carried his letter of resignation in his pocket, now dated and signed, and he was quite determined to tender it. Now that he was alone he was very certain that Mexico was his destination; he had a compelling desire to see Mexico, to meet and know first-hand the people who would—in three or four or five thousand years—send an army of occupation into the lost northern states.

The dormitory was bare, stripped of all but a bucket, and that bucket rested under a hole in the ceiling that had never been adequately repaired. Meltwater fell in a slow and steady drip, but no one had thought it worthwhile to make permanent repairs. The dormitory beds had been sent on to Sudbury on the same craft that had taken out the shop gear. They were needed, for many of the crew had been reassigned to that station. Debris was sighted there.

The small hospital room was equally bare.

Fisher Highsmith tarried there for long minutes looking at the spots where the two beds had been placed, where Seventeen and Eighteen had been brought together for a brief moment in time a thousand years distant from their home world. Two wasted antagonists from a lost battle, bitterly determined to fight a last battle in this alien place. They could not quit until one was dead. In his imagination Highsmith could still see the warrior's startling blue eyes glaring across the room and his adversary's soft brown ones watching *him* from the pillow. Neither pair had trusted *him*.

Harley and the hospital gear had gone on to Billings; Harley had flown out with the nurses, the two recoveries, and Jeanmarie. Harley had shaken hands in absent fashion and given his wife's address in Mexico—he'd said he was sure his wife would be pleased to see the reconstructionist. Jeanmarie had said goodbye with a polite touch, and walked to the aircraft clinging to Eighteen's hand.

The ready room was almost famiilar. His fine chair had once again been left behind.

The rug was taken up from the floor and the pilot's cot was gone grom the snoring corner; Jeanmarie's chair and the other few pieces of furniture had been removed and shipped to some other base, but his splendid ostrich-feather chair had been left behind for lack of space on outgoing craft, and now he wondered if it had originally been abandoned and left for *him* for the same reason. Had some long-ago flight officer also lost it because his people would not or could not find room for it on the outgoing freight? It was much too fine a chair to leave behind for the wolves and the storms to come.

Highsmith sat down in it and rocked back in easy relaxation. The chair moved with him in an equally easy motion, gently depressing itself to accomodate his spine and bony shoulders. They rocked together for a time while he stared at a blank space on the wall where the pictophone had been positioned. That blank space had never been painted. His legs stretched out carefully to find a place under the bench that was no longer there and he clasped his hands behind his head to contemplate the unpainted space.

He said aloud: "I wonder if that glow party is still going on in Billings?"

The voice of the sergeant bellowed in answer.

"Fisherman!"

The man was somewhere in the outer corridor, stalking through the nearly deserted base. The security officer was closing up shop.

Fisher Yann Highsmith obeyed the command and quit the ready room after a last look at his chair. He followed the sergeant and the corporal outside to the aircraft and climbed aboard, wedging himself into a seat surrounded by packing crates and remembering to plug in his heater cord. The pilot and two shop mechanics were aboard, all that remained of the base personnel other than himself and the military men. The pilot turned and glared at him for his tardiness. The corporal slid the door shut as the craft began moving along the snowy runway. A normal takeoff.

Highsmith scraped the frost from his tiny window and turned to look back at the empty, frigid buildings.

Someone had left the door ajar.